Air Within a Jade

TOMBALL COMMUNITY
WRITING PROJECT

Presented by Lone Star College-
Tomball Community Library
of
Harris County Public Library

Cover design by Kristina Deshee Magelky

Copyright © 2019
Tomball Community Library
All rights reserved.
ISBN: 9781096771715

DEDICATION

To the wonderful people of the Tomball community and greater Tomball area.

About the Tomball Community Writing Project

The Harris County Public Library (HCPL) system, based out of Houston, Texas, prides itself on providing its community with innovative services, programs, and outreach opportunities. The aim is, and always has been, to connect in meaningful ways with the community it serves, and to support its team members' efforts in this enterprise.

This proved to be the case when Lakisha Sparrow, Adult Program Specialist at the joint Lone Star College (LSC)-Tomball Community Library, decided to bring writing-based programming and services to the Tomball branch.

Sparrow successfully pitched a program idea to HCPL in the Summer of 2017, but she did not expect that her creative journey would take her onto a year-long enterprise of community partnerships, large-scale editing, and the compilation of the Lone Star College-Tomball and Harris County Public Library's very first Community Novel.

Sparrow's interest in the project started when she came across an article that discussed an innovative writing project started by a librarian, Lissa Staley, at a one-branch library in Topeka, Kansas. The project had been a novel, written by a small group of people, with each participant writing only one chapter, and the story unfolding as it went along. Immediately intrigued, Sparrow set out to investigate how this type of programming could be adapted, and what benefit the community would have by completing it.

Sparrow anticipated that the LSC-Tomball Community Library, one of 26 branches of the HCPL system, would be a great contender for the project. In fact, once releasing the project proposal to her colleagues and administrators at HCPL, there was a great deal of encouragement for its potential, and a great advocacy for the community involvement that would take place for the novel's completion.

The starting point would be to find out what, if any, interest the public would have for the project. In this respect, Sparrow was not disappointed, stating "I pretty much knew that I was not going to have trouble finding the twenty writers needed to make the book. I was right … in the first week I had a waiting list of interested people."

In a collaboration meeting in April of 2018, Sparrow was able to bring together the potential authors to discuss the novel, brainstorm ideas, go over the writing calendar and timeline, and start with a basic premise for the plot. Sparrow claims that this collaboration was integral to the community involvement and success of the project, saying, "It did help with the overall morale and sense of togetherness for the project … the meeting provided a sort of bonding among strangers. There were some people that held back at first, but came out of their quiet shells and provided ideas and comments."

The starting point was set, with Sparrow herself writing the first chapter and the participants moving the project forward thereafter, writing one chapter each before passing it off to the next writer. Sparrow edited the novel each week, and posted updates online, along with the biographies of each author as they wrote.

In addition to this process was a book cover contest, coordinated by Sparrow on behalf of the LSC-Tomball Community Library, which requested submissions for the cover design. Mrs. Kristina Deshee Magelky, the contest winner, completed the artwork featured on the cover in October 2018. As the design unfolded, there was great interest in showcasing as much of the cover art as possible.

Throughout the project, excitement remained steady amongst the Tomball community. That led to Community Novel project authors being featured in the Houston Chronicle, as well as being interviewed on 90.1 KPFT radio station's Living Art show.

The final completion of the work required the support from the Friends of the Tomball Community Library, who were greatly involved in the release of the novel as a self-published work available on Amazon, with proceeds going to the Friends group to fund further library programs and services. Sparrow embarked upon an extensive editing, revision, and upload to the Amazon 'KDP' site.

The end result of this enterprise came to a head in June 2019, with a soft release of the Community Novel's e-book. Titled *Air Within a Jade*, the Community Novel and its twenty featured authors, were launched to the general public.

Now, comes this final edition! On behalf of the Lone Star College-Tomball Community Library, Harris County Public Library system, and the Friends of the Tomball Community Library, we present to you *Air Within a Jade*.

Chapter One
by Lakisha Sparrow

"Is everyone ready?" The emcee's voice boomed from the speakers, as he stood in front of a band on the stage.

Affirmative answers were yelled in response from people throughout the ballroom.

"Then without further ado, it is time for the Charcoal Dance," he stated, and walked backwards offstage.

People started rising from their seats and went to the dance floor. Libby watched as they began to perform an interchange of traditional square dancing, and modern line dancing. A member of the band called out the moves during the square dance parts, and everyone seemed to know what to do for all of the line dance parts. It looked as though they had all rehearsed this for years.

And they probably had. Libby couldn't comprehend why she was slow to realize this. She counted this as the third element of the night that she did not know anything about.

There was a mysterious dance earlier where it seemed that attendees had to find someone wearing the same color as them, and take them to the dance floor to perform a modified waltz.

However, the dancers' adeptness had to be shown within two minutes, or they received a tap on the shoulder, and an escort off the dance floor. The skilled dancers that remained were eliminated until they were down to three couples, and the six of them received a trophy.

And there was also an interval where people were walking from table to table to exchange envelopes, and whisper things in each other's ears. Libby was clueless as to what any of these components were.

Right now, she was once again alone at her table, as she had been for practically the entire evening. Libby was at the Barbecue Ball — the exclusive, annual soiree of the small town of Atheneum. It was a celebration to mark the beginning of the extended summer heat that Texas is known for, and the months of outdoor food grilling that would ensue.

This was a masquerade ball, and everyone was required to wear a mask. Not just one over the top part of the face, but a full mask that actually hid the eyes, and the contour of the face. The most that anyone had out were their lips. The idea was for no one to really know who anyone else was at first glance. Even without masks, Libby still wouldn't know most of the people in attendance at the ball.

Since this special dance going on was yet another thing that Libby could not be a part of here, she decided to go to the restroom. The temperature in the ballroom was notably chilly, and she figured that was to try to even out the amount of heat that people would feel behind their masks.

This tactic was working well enough, but since she was being ignored anyway, Libby decided to go somewhere that she could take off her mask for a little more relief.

The large bathroom unit had fourteen stalls, and from what she could tell, it was empty when she entered. She grabbed some paper towels from the dispenser, wet them, and chose a large stall on the back wall. That way she could stand all the way in the back corner of it, without anyone being able to see her feet unless they actually looked under the stall.

She took off her mask and began to fan her face and the back of her neck with it. After dabbing her face and neck with the paper towels, she leaned her head back against the wall. Before she could even feel a modicum of relaxation, she heard women's voices as they entered the restroom.

They went to the sink and began talking about the enormous amount of fun that they were having.

"We have pulled off another successful rendezvous this year. The town's coordinators have never failed at pulling this together," said one of the women.

Libby was confused by what she had said. She didn't know if the woman was directly involved in the planning, or if she was taking credit just by being a resident of the town.

Libby surmised that there were only two of them, and she wanted to see who they were. Of course she didn't move, because she did not want to reveal that she was even in the restroom.

The conversation then took an interesting turn.

"How on Earth did that woman get past the front door wearing green," the same woman asked before giving a low, haughty laugh. "That is the ball's banned color for this year."

"Who is that anyway?"

"I'm not sure, but I think it's that woman that lives on that street. You know the one."

"Oh."

"That just goes to show that we can't just let anyone move here on a whim," was the final proclamation before they exited the restroom.

Libby kept her head on the wall and did not even try to fight back the tears. Crying was something that she had done a lot in the past two years. She couldn't make any sense of the mistreatment that she had endured since moving to Atheneum. She even felt like it was a battle just to attend this ball tonight.

It had to have been hundreds of times that she reflected back to what brought her here, and everything that she had done since then, hoping to find the clue that explained the reason for this abuse by the townspeople. There, sobbing in the stall, in her chartreuse dress, she speculated yet again.

She had been working at HouBayou Publishing for nearly two years, since the May of 2013. She was not only new to the town then, but to the state of Texas as well. Since the ball is held on the third Saturday of April each year, she arrived in town shortly after the 2013 occurrence, and no one was still speaking of the very private affair when she took up residence there.

In 2014, she still did not attend the ball. That year, at her job, and anywhere in town for that matter, she was being treated as an outsider. When she walked into places where 'privileged' subjects were being conversed about, talking automatically ceased. So, that year, she still had yet to hear of the Barbecue Ball.

This year, early in 2015, coworkers were beginning to get used to her presence enough that they were getting lax in their habits of ceasing conversations when she approached.

Taking advantage of overheard tidbits about the shindig, Libby felt safe in asking them questions about it. No matter the amount of boldness she felt in asking, she never got any direct answers from them. They easily ignored her, without any regard of whether they were being rude or not. Once questioned, they would seamlessly immerse themselves in a sudden task — copy-editing, looking at graphic designs, reading a manuscript. The brush-off was pretty much the same from each of them, as though it had been rehearsed for years. They would say, "Oh, dear. I've really got to get to this." That small declaration was like a special code.

After that, Libby instead used her research skills and prowess to find out about the ball. She found that, strategically, it had been constructed to only be attended by those who were born and raised in Atheneum. If you were raised there, but not still living there, you were required to still have a strong familial presence in the town. And it was difficult to get around that wall of kinship. Tabs were kept on all of the town's residents, including their whereabouts if they left.

Libby found out how serious it was when she went to purchase a ticket for the ball this year.

Her official address for the past two years was in Atheneum, so she felt that that was enough qualification for attending the ball. That matter itself was out of the ordinary, because the other contract employees have never lived in the town. The publishing company always refers them to a list of apartments in Gheldoux and Houston that are not far away.

The ball tickets were only sold at the town's Municipal Court, located on Main Street. Connected to the courthouse was the Tax Assessor's office, the City Council, and the Planning and Zoning Commission. This made it easy to have access of town birth and death records, house deeds, car registrations, and whatever else was needed to establish credential that someone was a verifiable long-term resident or descendent of Atheneum.

Libby had gone to a special office in the courthouse to purchase her ticket. There was a small waiting room there, with two adults and two children already seated. At the counter, she provided her driver's license, and informed the clerk behind the glass partition of what she came there for.

The elderly gentleman looked her up and down once, before settling on her face for several seconds.

"Have a seat," he said before getting up from his stool, and preparing to exit through a door on one of the side walls of his enclosed area.

Before he closed the door behind him, he had saw that Libby was still standing at the partition. More firmly this time, he repeated, "Have a seat," and did not close the door until she walked away.

That gave Libby time to have a glimpse at the area behind the door. She saw open shelves with manila folders lined up on them, with colored labels on the sides. They were reminiscent of folders that contain a person's medical records.

Unbeknownst to her, those folders were the unofficial tabs that were kept on the town's residents. The folders contained handwritten information about the town's residents, as well as pictures of them. For more than 115 years, the town's busybodies and gossips were responsible for the making of these records, even if they had no hand in actually penning any of it. It could be figured that the townspeople wanted to keep to its roots and original families, and found a way to build an invisible wall. Land ownership and property was passed down through the years, which made it easier to maintain the wall. And what better place was there to keep this unofficial information — in a building where official information is also kept.

Libby had not noticed a television in the small area where the clerk had been, but she could hear it playing. She could also tell that an episode of *The Andy Griffith Show* was on.

There were framed articles on the wall in the waiting area, and Libby decided to get up to read one while she was waiting. The one she chose was insightful. In the years that she had been there, she had never bothered to find out anything about the town's origins.

The article explained that around 1904, some railroad line engineers noticed that the area was on the boundary between the low hills of Texas and the flat coastal plains of the Gulf of Mexico, making it an ideal location for a train stop. From this region, there was a smooth, downhill coast, because the terrain gently sloped toward the Galveston ports. This meant that more cargo could be loaded onto railcars. A land prospector, Lorenzo Athens, who had a major role in the development of the Port of Houston, convinced the Essex-Knight Railway Company to run a line through the area. Soon after, the most was made of this new train stop. Houses, hotels, saloons, and mercantile stores were erected in the area, and the town was named Atheneum.

In another article, it was stated that in its 2.7 square mile land area, the population of Atheneum reached its maximum at a little under two thousand people in the mid-1980s, and has hovered at that number since then. The article boasted that the town has a minimal amount of shopping centers outfitted with chain stores, home décor shops, and electronics distributors.

    It went on to say that the purposeful tactic used was to build them as far outside of the heart of town that the boundaries would allow, and that has helped the inner Atheneum area in keeping its old look and feel. Even with asphalt on the street, it still can feel as though one is riding a buggy, being pulled by horses on a dirt road. This layout is one of the features that gives the town a distinct, close-knit feel among the bustling and sprawling cities of Gehldoux, Tomball, and Houston that border it.

    A man and woman entered the waiting room while Libby was still reading. The clerk reappeared at the window and greeted them warmly. He called over the other waiting family, gave them their four tickets, and they left. The man and woman approached the glass partition and exchanged small talk with the clerk while they called each other by name. The clerk eventually handed them their admission tickets for the ball, and they paid their fee. He had not even left his spot to get tickets for them, yet Libby was still waiting. After witnessing this, she could no longer concentrate on reading the articles.

    The couple said their goodbyes to the clerk, and he went back through his side door again. Libby sat back down and wondered why this town had such a strange desire to keep the old lineage, and bar non-natives from permeating its city limits.

This was even in effect at her job. HouBayou had a special entry-level program for recent college graduates that wanted to go into the publishing field. Through a staffing agency, three assorted positions ranging from editors, proofreaders, graphic designers, and marketing agents were offered on a two-year contract basis. The program and system had been in place since 1992, and is a valuable opportunity for those that are fortunate enough to secure one of the three positions.

Of the permanent staff members, there is a silent requirement that they all have to have been raised in Atheneum. No one vacates a position until they, or one of the other employees has a family member in the field that is going to take their place.

About three months before her contract was up, one of the permanent staff members, Hunter Valens, had to leave his Managing Editor position to take care of an ailing family member. At that time, Hunter did not have a replacement for himself, nor did any of the employees immediately have anyone to offer. Losing one editor would have increased the workload of each of the remaining editors and proofreaders, and would require them to have to work on weekends. But that wasn't as much of a consideration as was the fact that in order to keep the special funding that the company got due to having the contract positions, the publishing company was required to always have the position filled. Therefore, a job advertisement went out, and interviews were conducted.

Libby knew that there was no way that she was going to get hired permanently, but she decided to apply anyway. She was granted an interview, and throughout the questioning, she was regretful. Though she tried to concentrate, the same question kept running through her mind. *Why did I fill out that application?* And the same thought kept following her question. *You are never going to get this position.* She was sure that all of a sudden, some family member was going to show up, and be handed a shiny name plaque for their desk, and keys to the building.

Two weeks after her interview, with a little more than a month left in her contract, Libby was called into the office of her boss, Angela Lamar.

"Have a seat, Libby," Angela said while making a sweeping motion toward a chair facing her desk. Angela sat behind her desk and looked ready to get down to business.

Libby figured that she was going to receive the thirty days' notice of her contract ending. She scanned the desk for the usual gold jiffy envelope that she had seen given to other employees at the end of their contract. The envelope had always contained an acknowledgement letter of the contract's end, as well as recommendation letters from Angela, and the company owner, William Marquette.

But she didn't see the envelope there. She looked up at Angela, who was smiling. Angela's next words, *"We would like to offer you the position of Managing Editor,"* removed Libby's confusion, but replaced it with a significant jolt.

Libby started choking from the shock. Angela handed her a small water bottle from a cabinet in her desk.

"Are you alright?" Angela asked after the coughing subsided. Libby patted her chest a few times, and in a shaky voice, answered, "Yes."

Libby quickly got herself together. There had already been that nagging fear that someone else was going to swoop in take the open position. So although she was utterly dumbfounded by the news, she didn't want to have gotten this far and ruin it with this awkward display of physical emotions.

Angela informed Libby of everything that she was required to say and present when hiring a new employee, but Libby was barely able to focus. She was alert enough to confirm with Angela that she was accepting the position, and understood that follow-up paperwork would come later.

When Libby left Angela's office, she was still in utter shock. Her mind was trying to wrap around what had just happened, and she could not focus on her surroundings. She bumped right into the always-grumpy Wilson Jade, who of course had to be carrying a cup of hot coffee right then.

Although Libby was slender, she slammed into him with enough force to cause him to spill most of it — on himself.

"Ooooweee, ouch!" he exclaimed, and immediately began to fan the wet areas of his clothes with papers that he had been holding in his other hand. "Just look at my shirt and jacket," he continued to gripe while looking down at the brown splotches.

"I owe you a new suit," Libby said before bolting to the bathroom. There she could be alone, to try to quickly absorb what had just happened.

The clerk's voice calling her name brought Libby out of her reverie before her mind had the opportunity to go back a little further, and once again become saddened about the unpleasant way that she left her home in the southern part of Louisiana.

He was at the partition with her ticket. He drawled, "I'm sorry for the delay, but we weren't exactly expecting ... *you* to be purchasing a ticket. We hadda go get one printed." Libby had noticed that he slowly and more loudly said the word "you."

That had been yet another occurrence of the disdain that she battled on a nearly daily basis. She knew she hadn't done anything awful to anyone here. All she did was move here to take advantage of an opportunity for her career.

She was tired of having to brush off the bad treatment that she encountered, but what was she going to do? She had just accepted the permanent job position. She couldn't leave now, nor did she want to. That would have made her feel as though she would have to keep running each time life got a little disagreeable.

Before Libby had gotten the permanent position, she had avoided the thought so much that she had not even researched any companies in which she would have wanted to apply when her contract was up. Due to some advice that she took while in college to invest in cryptocurrency, Libby was privately wealthy. In her plans of that remaining a secret, she figured that she would have quietly stayed in her rented cottage for a few more months, and had hoped that no one would bother her.

Besides that, she did not really know where the money was. She turned over her initial investment funds to the other student that had advised her, and by the time she graduated, that student had informed her of the financial success. He gave her some paperwork and bank information that she still had, but she never looked at it again past that day. She didn't even know if her wealth was accruing, nor whether she was still involved in any aspects of it. She always figured that once she was out of the contract at the publishing company, she would take the time to find out what she needed to know.

Since that plan wound up being moot, Libby instead moved her focus to being what she thought was an official resident of Atheneum. The first step she felt was that going to this ball was going to force the townspeople to finally accept her, and stop treating her so crudely.

But here she was instead, crying in a bathroom stall. She wasn't even sure why their recognition mattered so much, other than that for some strange reason that she could not identify or pinpoint, she felt drawn to this town. The rest of the world was indeed open to her, but she did not feel that it was. She wanted to be in Atheneum.

Chapter Two
by Ollie Bream

After wiping away the tear streaks that her mascara left on her cheeks, Libby placed her mask back on, and left the fluorescently lit bathroom. She headed for the food table, as the distress caused her to seek some comfort food.

Everyone was busy dancing again, so they wouldn't notice one lone girl gorging herself on the multitude of pies that all of the women brought.

As soon as she picked up a plate and was debating about apple or cherry pie, she felt a light tug at the bottom of her dress. Libby looked down and was shocked when she saw a small child's hand poking out from beneath the food table.

"Shhh," said the young girl with a finger to her lips, "Mommy said to not leave Grandpa, but I got lonely. So what's your name?" the child asked inquisitively, as if she really wanted to know

Libby's name. Which was interesting considering that no adult had bothered that evening to even say hello.

"I... uh... I'm Libby. Short for nothing. Just Libby. Libby Ferguson." She was stuttering, which was very rare for herself, but she was really taken aback by this child in the midst of the ball.

"Nice to meet you, Libby. I'm Ruthie!" The little girl held out her hand with a level of maturity that Libby didn't know a child this young could possess. She wore a light blue dress the color of the sky, and sandals that displayed sparkly pink toenails. She looked to be about six years old.

"Would you like to sit with me and my Poppy?" Ruthie asked. "We're getting bored playing checkers in the back. He always lets me win, and he's fallen asleep so I went to look for other people who might play with me."

"Oh, I think you're mistaken Ruthie. I'm not alone," Libby responded. But who was she kidding, Libby was completely alone at the ball, would be completely alone when she went home, and also when she went back to work on Monday.

"Well yes you are! I haven't seen you dance with anybody yet!" Ruthie then proceeded to take Libby by the hand that was free from the empty plate, and dragged her to a table farthest from the stage and closest to the main doors. There was a warm breeze blowing through the open doors, and

Libby welcomed it right now as Ruthie tugged her. That was not to say that she minded heat though, for she had always loved summer. It reminded her of something that she couldn't quite put her finger on.

Ruthie sat down at the table next to a sleeping elderly man whose skin was worn like paper that had been wrinkled and thrown into the trash one too many times. Red veins rose to the surface of his cheeks and nose, and white hair made him look like he had the clouds resting on his scalp. He had a weathered look to his face. The deep, set creases at his mouth and eyes gave the impression that this man had known both great joy and great sorrow in his lifetime. In looking at him, Libby noticed that his head was rested on a bright *green* tie? Libby assumed that she had been the only one to not get the memo.   *Interesting*, Libby thought, but she wasn't sure why just yet. Libby sat down across from Ruthie, angling her body so she could see the dance floor where people swayed and bounced with one another in formation.

"My Mommy is the one in the pretty red dress," Ruthie pointed. She rested her head on her hands and watched the adults dance with awe. "One day, when I'm old enough, Mommy said that I could wear it!"

"I think that you would look really pretty in that dress Ruthie," Libby said as she spotted the woman that Ruthie's eyes followed. Her dress was really lovely, with a heart shaped off-the-shoulder bodice, and floor-length simple skirt that flew out from beneath the dancing lady.

Witnessing the elegant motion of this striking frock, it suddenly made Libby feel super self-conscious in her simple halter ball gown. Not to mention, it looked like everyone else had gone all out for their masks, by layering lace, flowers, glitter, and fabrics on them.

Libby's mask was light grey, and although she did use glitter as well, she had only used a light sprinkling of it that was barely noticeable. Except for when it annoyingly fell onto her lashes when she moved her head too much. Apparently, placing it on the eye area of the mask was a bad idea.

The music suddenly changed from a slow country song, to something that relied heavily on a banjo. This was bluegrass if Libby could remember from the one semester of 'Exploring Music' that she took in high school. She vaguely remembered that her instructor taught that there was a subtle distinction between bluegrass and rockabilly, but in this moment, she couldn't for the life of her, tell you what that nuance was. Whatever genre it was, it woke the old man, Poppy, up.

"Ah!" His eyes flew open, revealing the slightly opaque irises commonly found in old men.

"Ruthie? Ruthie, where are you? We haven't finished our game," he said before getting his bearings and seeing her there.

"Hi Poppy! How was your nap?" asked the sweet girl innocently.

"I wasn't napping missy, only resting my eyes. You know me, I like a good rest every now and then," a grin flickered across his lips.

"And who might this young'un be?" he asked when he noticed Libby at the table.

Ruthie scrunched up her face in confusion and asked, "Why are you calling her young'un? She's ol—."

"Hello sir, I'm Libby," she interjected, cutting off Ruthie's statement. "Short for nothing. Just Libby. I work at HouBayou Publishing."

She immediately pondered why she introduced herself with the name of her job.

"Don't call me sir, it makes me feel old," that grin flickered across his face again, but this time it looked mischievous. "I'm Poppy. What brings you to our humble table? Are you planning on running out with us? They won't see if we move fast enough."

Ruthie and the old man both smiled, his statement taking on the air of an inside joke between the two.

"Only if you'll let me," replied Libby with a small giggle. "Actually, I owe Miss Ruthie a big thank you. She rescued me from a mountain of calories over at the pie table that I surely would have regretted tomorrow."

The old man seemed satisfied with that response and his eyes left hers to look at the dance floor. He whispered something to Ruthie. She pointed to the woman in the red dress who was so entangled in the dancing that she didn't even notice her child or father staring straight at her.

Poppy looked intently at Ruthie and said, "I'm going to step outside for a little bit if you don't mind. It's gotten unbearably stuffy in here, and I think a bit of fresh air would do me some good."

In truth, the room felt just as comfortable as it had ten minutes ago, but the man seemed to have a mission and the little girl appeared content with that. That might have been because Ruthie was already occupied by colored pencils and paper that she seemed to have acquired out of thin air.

The old man started to raise himself out of his seat, but it was an immediate struggle. Libby didn't want him to stumble in his attempt to get out of the chair, so she rounded the table and gave him her arm for support. He took it and then looped their arms together. He led Libby out the front door into the humid night air.

Poppy sat on the top step with some help from Libby. He laid his blazer next to him and patted it as an invitation for Libby to sit beside him.

The garden was lovely that night, outside and away from the feverish beehive that was in the building behind them. It was quiet even though there were crickets and cicadas chirping in the bushes under the windows. The bright hues of the flowers were softened in the evening glow sponsored by the moon.

Poppy took a cigar from his breast pocket and lit it while Libby kicked off her silver pumps. Both adults breathed a sigh of relief at the fresh air and what also seemed like an immediate friendship.

"My wife once had a dress that exact color that you are wearing," he said as he stared out over the town of Atheneum. "No offense, but she really was the most gorgeous woman I've ever seen."

Libby laughed, "None taken." She tapped on her mask. "You don't even know what I look like."

"Touché."

After about a minute of silence, he sighed as if he was exasperated with something.

"Is anything wrong sir — I mean, Poppy?" Libby asked.

"Don't worry about it, Little Miss," he took a long drag of his cigar and flicked the ashes onto the cement next to him. "You wouldn't wanna hear a crotchety old man's opinion on life, my dear. Boring stuff really."

"I'm pretty sure it beats sitting alone at a ball no one wanted you at." Libby gently sighed and untied her mask. It was actually hotter outside than she had previously thought. Even though she knew it was not even important at this point, she still did not want more of her makeup ruined.

Poppy didn't even look her way as he continued. "Some of us old people here, we're like family heirlooms, only taken out once a year to show off to others. Tonight at this here ball, it's a bit of a show and tell really ... the most ostentatious affair this town sees, but it's once a year. After this, I'll be put away for safekeeping every other single damn day of the year. We are treated like we are babies. My daughter, my own daughter, talks to me the same way she talks to little Ruthie. But I know things," he said, "I know things about this town that they will never know unless they ask."

He grinned at that, like a teenager who successfully threw a party and didn't get caught. "And they'll never ask." Then Poppy just seemed to focus on something far off in the garden, wistfully stealing a moment to relish his secrets and hide his ... was it pride or was it shame? Libby couldn't tell.

Just before Libby could ask anything, someone walked out of the doors, saw the elderly man and young woman, and promptly walked back inside.

The person was young, wearing a dark navy suit, and frowning. He wasn't wearing a mask, and Libby saw that it was none other than Brandon Jade. Not one other person came out of those doors the whole time Libby had been talking to Poppy. Out of all of the people in attendance at the ball, the person that exited then was the worse person that could have.

He was Wilson Jade's brother, and he often came to Libby's job to visit Wilson. Brandon talked a lot, usually about other people's business. He often had to be nudged into silence by someone when Libby came around. This notorious gossip would probably begin spreading rumors immediately.

Brandon had interrupted a pleasant moment. Libby and Poppy were connecting, and Libby finally felt attached to something here after all of this time. Finally, someone in this town was talking to her, sharing with her, helping her feel like all of Atheneum wasn't against her. She was instantly intrigued in the secrets that the old man was alluding to, and the air of mystery he seemed to carry surrounding these secrets.

How much would he be willing to tell her? What are the secrets about the town of Atheneum, who never took in newcomers like herself?

At the same time, Libby felt a tinge of guilt, and thought that maybe she shouldn't be so eager for gossip or what could just be simple prattle.

Libby drew her gaze from the garden and looked to her left. Poppy was looking at her with an odd smirk. "You know that man, Brandon Jade?" he asked.

Libby gently nodded and sarcastically answered, "Of course I do, he's the Decaf Non-Fat Latte, one-and-a-half Splenda guy."

Poppy laughed and continued, "Well Mr. Non-Fat Latte Jade, he has dealings at Cairbow Development down the road from your publishing company."

Poppy paused to let Libby nod to the statement, affirming that it was true, she did know Mr. Jade and his reputation.

"He had big plans a while back to build a new community in the open space out on Northpine Road by the railroad," Poppy went on. "'An investment of a lifetime' was how he pitched it to the team and I. Little did that poor guy know that that land was owned by the state because it was the first piece of land that our town's founder Lorenzo Athens had gotten here. Or maybe he did. It's not like they teach it in History class anymore."

He sighed and inhaled his cigar. "It's a shame really. Kids knowing the history of the world but not of the very town they live in. If I had any say in it, kids would learn only their town history down to the names of each rat that lives in the original saloons," Poppy laughed good-naturedly at himself as smoke encircled his head giving him a halo.

He continued, "Although then we would have to tell them about the deals made in the darkest corners of the saloons on a "good word and a handshake ... back before everyone got their lawyer out to draw up papers to blow their own nose. The deals I'm talking about, well let's just say they weren't always so pretty."

"What type of deals?" Libby asked. She was enthralled now. To find out the history of the quiet town of Atheneum isn't so pretty — that's a thought!

"Oh you know, illegal subletting of property for profit of the owner. Gambling. The 'accidental' misplacement of someone's legal or family records in the town hall. Things like that. Things that don't matter now." Libby could tell that he was withholding some things that he really wanted to say. Certain incidents that had large impacts on the town, which he wasn't willingly handing over. And she wouldn't force him, as much as she wanted to know, as much as she yearned to open the curtains and shed some light on why she felt such a strong connection to this place, she couldn't and wouldn't force this conversation with this man she just met, this Poppy. This information wasn't her business.

She knew that it was wise for her to be apprehensive. Libby felt that if she attached to something or someone, it would be gone and Libby would be an outsider again. She took one last glance at the garden with its flowers and insects before she put her shoes back on her feet.

"Help me up, would you Libby," Poppy requested, and she got up and lifted him with his right arm, and then handed him the jacket he let her sit on for their conversation.

"It was lovely meeting you Libby. Don't be a stranger now. I visit the library some Monday afternoons," Poppy announced.

With that, he walked back into the dance hall, and left Libby to speculate about things he just said. Along with the other aspects of her life that she was already dealing with, Poppy's conversation had already added more questions in her mind.

One statement from him really stood out, though — he made sure to tell her when he would be at the library.

Chapter Three
by L. Piper

Libby glanced out the living room window as she opened her laptop. The sun was just starting to rise, and the pine trees outside were just gaining color. Through the spaces between their tall trunks, Libby could see the railroad tracks glinting in the new light. She smiled as she looked at them, but quickly moved her focus back to the computer. Otherwise, she knew that she could get lost staring at them for hours.

She logged into the group feed for HouBayou Publishing, and a dull feeling washed over her. She'd spent the hour before bed last night typing up book recommendations on the company's public media page. It'd been a bit of fun, posting her short reviews. She had recommended eight chilling summer reads to ease the heat of another Texas summer.

But her posts had been deleted.

On her My Account page, there were notifications of activity after she posted her recommendations. She clicked on the different people's names shown there, and saw that some of the male readers had commented and attached tiny red hearts beneath Libby's words.

But in the chatroom page, their likes and hearts, along with the recommendations were gone. Mild anger settled over her. As this was a required assignment, she checked the recommendations from the other HouBayou employees. Those were all still as they had been when she'd read them last night.

Meow-meow-meow-meow-meow.

Libby looked up. "Greystoke. You're early," she said, the cat's arrival a welcome interruption from the bad train of thoughts that had entered her head.

She got up from her little desk and went to the kitchen to make breakfast for her visitor. The little three-legged cat had taken to hanging on the window screen next to her desk sometime over the last few months. Libby identified with the gray, furry animal. She felt that they were both hanging on to the fringes of life.

In the kitchen, Libby poured out kibbles in a bowl, and mixed a cut-up cat vitamin throughout the food. Ready for her morning walk, she took that, along with a bowl of fresh water to the porch. She grabbed her fanny pack, locked up, and went through the backyard fence to access a trail that led to the railroad tracks. It was Saturday, and she always took longer walks on the weekends since she did not have to go to work.

While walking on the charcoal-colored rocks alongside the rails, she thought about whether it was weird to like living by railroad tracks. She didn't mind the loud horn — not even at night when she was sleeping. It only occasionally woke her up, and when it did, she was able to easily fall right back asleep.

Whenever her mind went to the posts that had been deleted, she forced herself to stop thinking about it. There had to be an explanation for it, especially since it was not something that she just arbitrarily decided to write. To put her mind on something else, she pulled a memo pad out of her fanny pack, wrote a shopping list, and a To-Do list for the week.

The To-Do list was a joke. How much did she have going on in her life that she had to keep track of? Wake up while it was still dark, take a walk at sun-up, go to work, come home, read a book or magazine, occasionally watch tv, and go to bed. There was hardly any variance from this routine, and that was only the random weeknights that she chose to shop for food or other necessities. She avoided going shopping on weekends because she did not like the large amounts of other people there. She was fine with crowds in other aspects — concerts, sporting events — but just not while shopping.

An hour out and already on her way home, the tension and negativity had given way to make room for the weight of beauty from the birdsongs. The beautiful dance of the wind in the tree branches, glimpse of frogs and lizards resting in the nook of a tree root.

Almost home, the block before her cottage, Libby left the tracks to walk down Holt Street to get a cold soda at Thirp's Feed Store.

The man running the store, Fred Thirp, nodded at her when she came in. After she'd put her coins into the soda machine and reached for the cold can that fell into the tray, Thirp said "Take care now."

"Thank you. You too, take care." His slight kindness made her feel teary, it was the tiniest of pleasantries and such a sharp contrast to seeing her words erased from the chatroom at HouBayou.

Exiting Thirp's, wind jerked the screen door from Libby's hand. A great sweep of cool air, unusual for this time of year in Atheneum, blew her clothes tight against her body and pulled her hair free from its loose tie. Once on the wooden steps of the feed store, Libby took a deep breath of the chilled air, then all-at-once, Libby was no longer in Atheneum.

The sky which had been a brilliant blue, was now a roiling mass of grey-black clouds. Libby was no longer a woman on the steps outside Thirp's, she instead was a little girl on a ship out at sea. Gone was the moist soda can in her hand. Instead, the little girl clutched a brown teddy bear tightly by its little arm.

She wasn't supposed to be up on deck, but she couldn't sleep and had come up to get Aunt Melanie to tuck her in. She loved her aunt. And even though it was very bad, she often wished she was Aunt Melanie's little girl.

Suddenly a huge wave crashed over the side of the boat. The girl with the teddy bear slipped and fell, her feet going straight out behind her. She landed flat on her stomach, wetting the bear and her clothes. Wind that roared in her ears, and thunder blotted out the shouts of her mother and aunt.

Libby had hurt her knee and she wanted one of the women to notice. "Mommy. Auntie Melanie," she whispered, and raised her teary eyes to see them come to her. Instead, what she saw made her pain worse and her whole body trembled. They were fighting. Striking each other. She thought she said it but maybe she didn't — "Don't fight. Please — please don't fight."

The boat pitched hard and sent Libby sliding sideways on the deck. In the moonlight, she saw something gleaming in the hands of the women.

There was a loud bang, louder even than the thunder, and so close that the little girl's ears hurt. She smelled smoke like at the fireworks of the July picnics that she always went to. Then everything lit up as blue-white lightning cracked across the length of the black clouded skies.

"Ruthie? Ruthie?" Libby asked the person in front of her.

"Lib? Libby? I said, are you okay?" Jane stooped and picked up Libby's lime soda which had fallen on the scraggly patch of grass in front of the gravel parking lot of Thirp's.

Jane continued with her questioning. "Who's Ruthie?"

Libby shivered and blinked, then recognition settled onto her face. It was Jane Farrell, a woman she met a few months back while shopping at the Farmer's Market in Gheldoux, but had not seen since. Jane did tarot card readings and sold herbs in a small trailer a few blocks away from Libby's house in Atheneum.

She and Libby had fallen into a conversation after buying coffee at one of the stands. They sat at one of the picnic tables there, and Jane informed Libby of her occupation. Libby told her about the strange dreams that she had been having. She gave Libby her business card and a couple of suggestions, and told her how she could be of further help.

"I'm sorry," Libby shook her head like she was still trying to get rid of the images.

"Stress from work?" Jane asked.

"No," Libby said. "I almost wish it were that simple. It was another of those dreams I told you about before. I had just walked out of the store, and the next minute I was somewhere else. I'm a little concerned. What if it happens while I'm driving?" But before Jane could say anything, Libby answered herself. "It probably only lasted a minute, if that. Tell me I'm just being silly. Right?"

"If bothers you it's not silly, and you do have reason to be worried," Jane said with genuine concern on her face. "That is a good point that you brought up about the possibility of it happening while you are driving. Even five or ten seconds could be detrimental. I don't even want to think of a whole minute.

"I can make you up some lavender herb sachets. One for your pillow and another for your car," she continued. "If it's just stress, they'll help. Did you start keeping a journal like I suggested before?"

Libby beamed and patted her fanny pack. She was delighted that Jane remembered something from their past meeting. "I did. I actually have it right here." Although it was just some notes that she jotted down in the memo pad while on her daily walks, it still had the information needed.

"Maybe you should come for a reading right now, and I can give you the sachets also," Jane said.

*****

At Jane's trailer, the women faced each other across a table covered with a dark cloth. A light wind rattled the windows of the trailer, though the flame of the candle between them never flickered.

"Shuffle the cards," Jane said, and handed Libby a thick deck of cards larger than regular playing cards.

As she divided and shuffled the sections back together, Libby wondered if she was about to solve the whole mystery of the recurring dream that she kept having. She finished and handed the deck back to Jane.

Jane held the deck of cards with both hands. "State your first question," Jane said.

"Why am I here?" Libby said.

Jane followed up Libby's question with her own inquiry. "Here at my trailer, here in Atheneum, or here in life in general?"

"Ummmmm…" Libby felt foolish as she realized that her question was too broad.

Jane helped ease her mind. "Actually, you should refresh my memory about these sudden dreams that you have."

Libby told her about the dream, and also informed her that it didn't always happen in the same place. It was always a fight between her mother and her aunt, but the location varied from a boat, an amusement park, a ski lodge, and even an airplane. Libby told her she thought that other nonsensical locations could also come up in the future.

She told Jane that the dreams started about a year-and-a-half ago, and had no regular occurrence. That would have made more sense to her, if they happened on regular intervals like once every six weeks, three months, or 4th Tuesday. Anything that could help her expect them and prepare.

She flipped through her memo pad and told Jane that once she could not find any fixed intervals, she went back and looked at her work logs. There she noted that it seemed a dream occurred whenever she received a manuscript that featured women that were best friends, or had some other type of non-familial long history.

"And speaking of work, I remember that you mentioned that you had some problems there," Jane said. "Give me that run-down again."

Libby told her about her time there, and even mentioned last night's posts.

After deliberating Libby's history there, Jane reasoned, "It doesn't really sound like people have been especially mean to you. They just don't seem to be willing to build friendships with you."

Libby pondered this for a few moments and said, "From tv and movies I just thought that people made friends at their workplace, had lunch together, sometimes hung out after work and on weekends. I guess I just had a bad prototype. Now I know that things don't always turn out that way."

Jane spread out the cards in a u-shape. She told Libby to run her hands over the cards, and pick out the card that she felt most compelled to. Libby picked one and sat it to the right of her. Jane directed her to mix up the cards again and then place them in a stack to establish a unity.

The first card that Libby then chose from the pile was called the Significator card, and she placed it in the center of the table. Jane said that it directly represented Libby herself, or the question that she had. She had not, however, even established a better question after her first broad one.

Jane flipped over the next card. She said that it dictated the appearance of anyone being questioned by the subject or the subject themselves. There were two dark-haired women on the card. Then there was a fair-headed woman on another card, which she said represented someone more inquisitive, keen, quick-witted, and logical, trying to balance things out in her own head and strength within her own life.

More cards were flipped and placed on the table, and Jane gave explanations for them. "This card has to do with the past, and also of embarking on new ventures without hesitation … a sense of dullness … one wants to enterprise further quickly … the card that crowns goes with the foundational card … influences to come … the base of the wand … sending someone to represent you in an undertaking … here to take you on a journey … family influence … next card up … sudden misfortune … pleasure in the simple life … gaiety and light-heartedness … the sun, the place of hopes …"

Libby had taken several English Literature courses in her college studies, and was used to analyzing and finding hidden meanings. She knew all about symbolism, themes, motifs, and different forms of literary theory. She was trying to keep up and understand what Jane was telling her.

At the end, four cards were vertical on her left side, with four cards in the middle forming a square, and more vertical and horizontal cards above that, and on the right.

"I think that is enough to think about for now," Jane said as she scooped the cards back into a messy pile. "If you want to schedule regular readings, like once every week or two weeks, just let me know."

"I sure will," Libby said before Jane quickly jumped up from the table, and grabbed her smartphone from her purse. She stood in a corner with her back to Libby, but Libby could tell that Jane was frantically scrolling on the screen, and typing intensely.

"I can just walk home if you're busy. That seems important." She didn't want to appear impatient, but since it was obviously something that Jane did not want her to see, she couldn't understand why Jane didn't wait until she was gone.

"No, no. I've got it taken care of. I'll drive you home now." Jane walked back toward Libby and the door, but did not look at her.

After Libby had first met Jane and found out that they lived close to each other, she had hoped that they could become friends. When she saw her outside of the feed store, she was happy and hopeful to pick up where they left off at the Farmer's Market in a non-client relationship. But after agreeing to the reading today, that didn't seem possible. How would they be able to cut the business relationship now that one had pretty much been established?

Libby said her goodbyes to Jane in her driveway, and went into her house. After making a snack, she went to her desk. Her laptop was still opened, and she refreshed the HouBayou Recommendations page.

Weirdly, her original posts were back, along with any likes and comments that she had received. She checked her work email, and saw that there was an apology from Angela Lamar about the "accidental" deletions. Libby noted that Angela's email was only three minutes old.

Since she spent so much time alone, Libby frequently used it to question a lot of things in her mind. Out of that normal habit, she wondered whether it was an innocent coincidence that she ran into Jane today? Now that there was the possibility of a budding friendship with Poppy and finding out about Atheneum's secrets, why had Jane suddenly shown up again? And why did she just notice today that the little girl in her sudden daydreams looked like Ruthie?

Chapter Four
by Elizabeth Sheridan

The piercing shrill of a six-thirty morning alarm was enough for Libby to sit bolt upright. Blankets were strewn about the bed, and Libby was gasping for air, a fine sheen of sweat on her brow. She caught sight of herself in the mirror on the opposite wall, and struggled for a moment to get her bearings. What she saw was the after-effects of another nightmare.

Greystoke appeared at the foot of her bed, and with a skeptical glance her way, began to complain loudly about not being fed. He helped bring Libby back from the remnants of another one of those strange dreams to the bright surroundings of her bedroom. She had a dryness in her mouth, and a dull, sluggish headache.

"Hey buddy," she said, and pet Greystoke's head for a moment until she caught her breath. Despite the early hour, the day was already bright. Through a crack in her curtains, Libby could see sunlight and a blue sky. Normally Libby woke up while it was still dark. Even as she set the alarm on her cell phone last night, she was certain that her internal alarm would wake her up at her usual time. She didn't think that she was actually going to sleep the additional two hours that she keyed in.

She closed her eyes briefly, stretched her neck, and rolled her head to clear it. But Greystoke was loudly determined to get his food. With a sigh, Libby threw back the bed covers and got up.

In the small kitchen, she put kibbles down for Greystoke, and fixed a dark cup of instant coffee. The hot liquid warmed her tongue when it hit her throat. Now that she had quieted the cat, she closed her eyes again, and rubbed her neck and temples.

Once she felt some relief, she opened her eyes. They went straight to the counter where the same newspaper sat for the past four weeks. On its cover, the words ANOTHER UN-BALL-IEVABLE ATHENEUM NIGHT! yelled at her in black. A photo took up the spread. It was an older, graying, well-suited man. He was wrinkled, but debonair. Next to him was the smaller frame of a woman about the same age, her hair neatly placed in an updo, earrings and necklace sparkling around her face. Written at the bottom of the shot in small black print: *Mr. and Mrs. August Jade showcase another beautiful evening at their palatial estate.*

Libby decided it was finally time to get rid of the paper, and she dumped it next to the litter box. She wished she could no longer remember the night of the ball, and keeping such a vivid reminder was not a logical idea.

From the living room window, the railroad tracks glinted through the thick tree trunks, and beckoned her for a walk. She dressed quickly, grabbed her keys, and dumped the remainder of her coffee into a green travel mug with a HouBayou Publishing logo on the side. Within minutes she found herself on the trail leading to the tracks.

The smell of earth and trees was thick — perhaps that was the appeal of 'walking the line.' It was a well-used line, to be sure, but the trains were intermittent enough that the track was clear most of the day. There was an easy slope on either side, and before reaching the dark green trees, the expanse was wide, with trains easy to spot. Libby took easy steps toward Holt Street and Thirp's for a coffee refill. Her mind wandered far easier with her headache fading, and the thought of entering a store where somebody would quip a happy 'Mornin'.' It was a change to see a smiling face, especially in this town.

As it had many times before, Libby's mind turned to Atheneum with its older buildings and traditional families. What was it about this town? She'd been many times before to Gheldoux, not three miles west of here, and things were so very different. So much so, that Libby had considered a move there. For the time being, Libby had opted to stay in Atheneum. The town itself was beautiful to look at. Small homes, quaint and well-kept, surrounded charming official buildings. Christmas here was a sight to behold too, with decorated lamp posts and store fronts. The town was a postcard picture perfect for a *Kinkade*.

Yet, there was a dullness here. A subtle wrong about the place. At first, Libby thought that it was her newness to the area. She was an outsider and small towns had their way. But it had been two years since her arrival, and still, the aloofness of her neighbors puzzled her.

For more than an hour Libby meandered the line, pausing for long breaks every so often. She walked further in one direction that she normally did. She was occupied by her thoughts and the softness of the morning — forgetting altogether about Thirp's. She had nowhere to be this Monday, as she had given herself a three-day weekend. There was going to be a promotional opening for a new, unremarkable publication tomorrow, and she wanted a little break before that. Libby wondered briefly whether her clothes for the event would make her stand out as much as she had at the ball. Or whether that would happen by its own accord, through her meagre presence.

She would have stayed on the line, happily walking the morning away, but a gap in the trees showed a large blue and white square sign, posted stubbornly by the side of the road running parallel to the tracks: LIBRARY.

It had been years since Libby had been in one, since leaving college in fact, and the sign made her smile. It brought back memories of studying late, and sneaking bites of pizza behind piles of books. She felt this sign was new, as she did not remember seeing it any other time that she walked on the railroad tracks. Something about its existence appealed to her. She found herself following the road a full block to a surprisingly sheen, metallic building with respectably large windows, and a pretty rose garden. It was the complete opposite to every official building in Atheneum. Its sleek doors opened automatically, and a large and happy sign with a cheery flower logo was posted to the right:

Atheneum Public Library
Open Hours: 8am–8pm Mon–Fri,
Sat 10am–5pm

Inside, the room was circular. The cool, crisp air made her chill quickly, but something pleasant about the smell of the books resonated. They lined the stacks in a neat, symmetrical movement around the walls. The shades at the tall windows filtered the sunlight to create a happy glow. The order appealed to Libby.

"Morning!" chirped a hidden voice. "I'll be right with you. So sorry. Apparently opening the doors this morning pushed the computers too far, they overloaded and quit on us." The voice came again from below a desk to Libby's left.

Within seconds though, an echoing beep bounced off the walls, and the computers made a whirring sound of life.

"Hello. Sorry 'bout that." The librarian who emerged from underneath the desk was a rainbow. Blue hair swept beautifully upward into a sparkly clip, orange chunky earrings brushed against a tie-dyed scarf wrapped around the neck of a woman, whose green eyes flashed behind black-rimmed glasses.

"You look like you need directions," she said in clipped tones. She looked no older than thirty, but something in her manner reminded Libby of her high school principal who had little time to waste, and who clicked around the halls hastily in impossible heels. Both the principal and the librarian were all business.

"Morning." Libby chuckled "Ummm, yes, I suppose I do. I haven't been to a library since college."

"Well, welcome back, glad to see you," said the librarian. Her name tag said 'Daisy' and she had a wide, gummy smile.

"Get the layout yet?" she asked, but did not wait for Libby to answer. "Fiction is behind me, Non-Fiction behind you, Children's to the left, Periodicals and Checkout to the right, bathrooms are at the back. Need a library card?"

"Ummm, sure." Libby was happy to see a smile emerge from Daisy.

"Fill out this application, bring it back with your ID card, and we'll get you set up," Daisy directed Libby. "Here's a pen."

Libby hadn't thought about frequenting any library at all since college, but since her list of allies in this town seemed short, it was nice to have someone to talk to.

"Thanks," Libby said, and took the crisp paper over to a nearby table.

The only sounds coming from her immediate surroundings were the tapping of computer keys. Daisy sat poised and straight-backed at her desk, rustling papers with one hand, and holding a stack of six books in the other as a waiter would hold a tray of plates. A couple sat at couches behind her. Every so often the man would chuckle and look up and around for someone to share his laugh with, but it wasn't the woman sitting next to him. Instead she was reading a book about crochet, and her fingers were fidgeting, weaving wool that wasn't there.

From a hall to Libby's immediate left, she caught the drift of swing music and happy voices. There was also a set of stairs and a small elevator that Daisy had not mentioned. Libby stood and wandered over, noticing that next to the stairs and down the hall, there were pictures on the walls; large, black and white, with silver frames.

On another day, she may have passed them without looking, but the familiar landscape in one of the photographs made her stop. It was the courthouse. In the photograph, three very dapper gentlemen stood either side of a clock face, which was on the ground outside and was obviously the last addition to some building. A woman stood to their side, her voluptuous dress frilled out of the frame, and her bonnet shadowed her face. Below the scene on the bottom left of the picture, white ink marked the page.

Left, Wilbur Jade Snr., Bros. Cody Jade and Otto Jade hold finished clock face. Moira Hackley, right. Municipal Courthouse, 1913.

This was the Jade family. Maybe the original Jade family of Atheneum, Libby thought. Her mind then reached to Wilson Jade and his brother

Brandon. Wilson had worked with Libby for the past two years, and that was a work relationship she could have done without. He was watchful, then critical, then smug. His pinched, pale face and beady eyes were a constant in the office. His brother Brandon was younger and far more handsome. Sandy colored hair and wide blue eyes, and an easy smile. But, Brandon's presence in the office with his brother spelled trouble. He seemed to know everything, about everyone. Libby had been in Atheneum not two days before they'd first met.

His cool eyes had appraised her quickly. She had been dressed for work, nothing too smart, and his eyes lingered on the Louboutin shoes she'd worn. They were a gift she'd given herself for the new job. Both of those Jades knew expensive taste, both men were a force in the town. It was their family who had bought almost all of the stores in Atheneum and in Yearborough, which was a shanty-town oil field five miles away going north. The flat expanse of outlet stores on the new paved road which led east of here belonged to them too. They were old money, in an old town, and they weren't going anywhere soon.

The photograph on the wall told the same story going back generations. The three men in the picture were overbearing, the same cool eyes as Wilson's and Brandon's reached out of the frame at Libby. The woman looked very much like many of the women in the town — pale skin, wide hips, and curly golden hair. Libby wondered why it was that this seemed to be. Her dark, straight hair and deep brown eyes were unusual here. While their body types were mostly pears, she had a tubular shape. She did not have the Atheneum look.

Standing in front of that picture, an idea came to her suddenly, and she wandered back to Daisy at her desk.

"Finished?" Daisy asked smiling.

"Yes, thanks for that. I have another question, maybe you can help."

"What I'm here for," Daisy smiled wider.

Libby hesitated, but then said, "I'm looking for a history, on the town. Something that would tell me about how it was founded, and maybe something about the people here. She added, "Something on major events?"

Daisy's green eyes flashed mischievously behind her glasses. "Ah," she said, "you are after that."

Her eyes wandered to the staircase. "What you are looking for is on the second floor, in Reference. It's called Atheneum: Town History, Tribulations, and the Social Ethos of the Bygone Echelons."

Daisy took a minute to scribble on a small square scrap of cream-colored cardstock. Her writing was a neat cursive, and when she passed the card to Libby, the book's title was written there with a code: REF 976.4 Uld.

"It's on the second floor," she repeated, "took a lot to keep it there too. That's why it's Reference. Can't check it out, but you can make some copies. Tends to walk off the shelf if we have it openly available."

These last words, Daisy said slowly with a nod of her head, and a knowing stare over the rims of her glasses.

Libby didn't quite know what that meant, but took the card gently from Daisy's fingers and said, "Oh. Okay, well thank you very much."

"Welcome. Numbers are at the end of the shelves, it's a small section."

"Thanks again."

The climb upstairs meant that the temperature increased. The second floor was circular too, but cut in half by a wall with a red sign: Staff Only. To the left was another sign which said Special Collections in a shiny gold font, and to the right REFERENCE.

Libby walked toward large wooden shelves and noticed the neatly printed numbers at the end of each. 200s Religion, 500s Sciences, 900s History. She wandered down the gap between this last stack, until she reached the book — a thick flat spine in grey, with the bold white letters Atheneum.

Libby gingerly lifted it from its place and brought it to a round table in the open space between the collections. She rubbed her hand over the glossy cover on which there was printed a picture of Main Street, probably from about a hundred years before Libby had even thought about living here. The name of the author, Grant T. Uldrich, was in neat blue at the bottom.

"You're not going to actually read that rubbish are you?" said a raspy voice from behind her, which made her jump.

Turning, she caught sight of the speaker and immediately smiled. The white hair and twinkly-eyed face of Poppy smiled back at her.

"Ain't nothing in there that will tell you anything." He waggled a bony finger before the book, and chuckled. "What you need is more coffee."

"More coffee?" Libby chuckled, realizing that he was referring to the tumbler that she was holding.

"Yup," Poppy said. "Come on. I told you I'd be here, but I started to believe that you wouldn't ever come. Since you are finally here, we're heading to the place where things really matter. The Corner. Bring the book."

And just like that, he was disappearing down the stairs.

Libby hesitated only for a second or two before she heard his voice echo back up from the staircase, "Catch up!"

Grabbing the book, she followed.

Chapter Five
by Genova Boyd

The corner turned out to be The Corner, an open design coffee shop attached to the library, and clearly the place that most visitors congregated. Libby slipped the book to her side, unsure whether or not it was meant to be removed from the shelf at all. Poppy was already ordering from a tall teenager with spotty skin, and a hat with the American flag on it.

"Two black coffees, biggest size you've got."

Turning to Libby he said, "Creamers over there." He pointed to a bench by the windows with spoons, sugar packets, and a line of sticky syrup bottles. "They don't charge extra for those."

Libby took her cup and thanked Poppy. She sat and looked around her while he took his time adding a dark brown syrup and a thick bunch of sugar packets to his hot drink. There were a group of young people in the corner who were on their phones, but obviously playing a game together. They tilted their screens at the same time, and all seemed engrossed in the glowing images before them. A couple held hands over their coffees at a table near the sweeteners — he was reading something to her, and she was rubbing her thumb across his palm. The barista was leaning across the counter, talking to two other friends on the other side. They had a stack of lapel pins in front of them and were playing some kind of swap game with them.

The whole scene was such a stark contrast to anything Libby had experienced of the town before. This happy little coffee shop at the back of the library was the most jovial place Libby had seen in two years. It was a sad thought, but Libby felt like she'd stumbled on some kind of a Mecca.

Poppy sat opposite, appraising her with twinkly eyes. "Bit of light reading?" he pointed to the book between them.

"Yeah, I guess. I don't know. I saw a picture in the hall there with the courthouse, and I thought …"

Libby paused for a moment, thinking diplomatically about her next words. "I thought it might help me to learn about the town … about its history … so that I can get a feel for it a bit better. Ummm … fit in better, I guess."

Poppy began chuckling. "Yeah," he said in a deep baritone. "I can see how you'd think that, but I'm sorry to tell you that it ain't gonna work."

He took a long sip of his coffee and Libby glanced down at the book. It was a thick tome. She thumbed the paper, and flicked the corners. She stopped when she came to a picture of four men wearing overalls and boots, covered in black oil. She silently estimated that it was probably taken sometime in the 30s.

"I can tell you," said Poppy pointing at the picture, "I can tell you what it says in that book."

"Oh yeah?" Libby smiled.

"People don't listen to us old folks, and only want us to come out once a year with our ties on." He pointed to his. It was the same bright green one he'd had at the ball, only Libby hadn't noticed until then that it had been cut at the bottom. Snipped clean across to make a sharp blunt end.

"What happened to your tie?" she giggled, and he laughed back.

"Yeah. Green was not the color to wear to the ball this year," he said with continued amusement. "It was not intended for everyone, but there was a certain color that was meant to be worn and stand out. Didn't you notice?"

Now that Libby thought back, she realized he was right. A lot of women at the ball had worn a shade of red. And regardless of what color suit they were wearing, there was an abundance of men that had on red ties. It had been her and Poppy in green that had been outcasts.

"That's the thing with this town," Poppy's smile faded slightly, "those that run the town set the rules, big or small. And the others follow. If you are meant to wear red, you wear red. Which I did have on when I left the house. But I changed to this green tie in the backseat of the car. I knew my daughter would be too excited to notice when we got to the ball. August and his wife were greeting attendees at the door, and they looked at me with the most furious of sour looks possible. My daughter turned around to see what was causing this, and her mouth flew agape with a smack. Under her mask, I know her face was redder than her dress. I just walked past the three of them, and started mingling. But during one of the times that I was 'resting my eyes,' my daughter came and cut my tie!" he laughed heartily. "Thought I'd take it off. No siree."

He laughed some more. "Well, not right then anyway. I took it off when I wanted to use it as a pillow, but put it back on after you'd left. I didn't get rid of it that night, and I'm gonna keep wearing it, just because she did it. It's silly, I know, but it makes her so mad, and keeps me laughing and young."

Libby smiled and took a sip of coffee. She noticed the color of his tie at the ball, but didn't notice the slice in it as his head was resting on it that night. She asked "What do you mean when you say 'those that run the town set the rules?' I know that the Jade family are old money here, but who else?"

"Hmmm," Poppy swallowed a mouthful of creamy, sugary liquid and looked at her thoughtfully. But then he started, and when he did, he spoke for some time.

"Although not in name, Atheneum was really founded by four families. They were the Eulers, the Threadgoods, the Sleuths, and the Jades. They found oil in Garrop Valley not far from here."

"In Gheldoux by any chance?" Libby asked.

"That's it," Poppy replied. "The four families had been here working the land together since the turn of the century, before striking the liquid gold in the nearby valley. Rumor has it that they all came here because the Atakapa Indians told them that there was oil around here, but no one knows how they knew it for sure. Back then, after they got the oil, Lorenzo Athens advised about the rail line.

Poppy took a slow sip of his coffee this time before continuing. "The four families paid homage to him by allowing the town be named after him, even though they were already there. They probably inherently thought about how his idea had the potential to make them some money, and they also would not have to spar about which family moniker would be used.

"They started building and not long after, others came. First, the ones that were needed. More labor for the land and such ... then butcher, baker, broker, law man, you name it. The town boomed in a few short years.

"Now the Eulers were already a wealthy family, far more than the rest of them, because of their financial ties to vineyards back up in Fredericksburg. They wanted to keep their family together after coming over from Germany. So, when time came to leave and go back to Fredericksburg, the Jades bought them out. Not for cheap either. Pretty much wiped the Jade family clean of everything that they made with the oil, to acquire all of the Euler share. But they did anyway, and it wasn't long after that they made it all back with all of theirs, and the Eulers' land and minerals."

Libby stirred her coffee, but kept her eyes transfixed on Poppy while he continued to speak.

"And the Threadgoods and Sleuths didn't like that at all. See, they were all now wealthy from the oil, but the Threadgoods and Sleuths felt that they were somehow more established than the Jades," he stopped and shrugged his shoulders. "Why? Don't ask me. But Jade money was considered new stock. It made a difference back then.

"Well, the Threadgoods started buying up land around the oil — they could afford that see?

But it was in Gheldoux. The Sleuths took over the roads, all the buildings, and attracted people here. They even extended the rail line east, and erected an end stop in Threadgood territory. That last part was a benefit for both families. And it all looked fine, until about 1906, when it became clear to the Jades that the Threadgoods and the Sleuths had a monopoly."

Poppy was becoming animated; his eyes were bright and his hands moved about him enthusiastically. He flipped to a picture in the book, a small black and white print of the early train station. It looked like the one that Libby passed every day on Westleigh Road.

"See everything that came in and out of the town," said Poppy, pointing to the picture, "had come in through road or rail and it had to be stored somewhere. Well, that was all the Sleuths. Any attempts to expand the oil business meant that land had to be bought, and that belonged to the Threadgoods. The more that the Jades tried to gain, the more that the Sleuths and the Threadgoods pushed back. Boy, if they'd been successful, they may have been the ones running the town.

"But, then the Great Depression hit and Threadgood money dried up. They had put most of into investments and lost it all. They had to sell up. Eventually recovered though. Ended up north in the Carolinas, building bridges, and made another fortune.

"But the point is, that they sold their land — half to the Sleuths and half to the Jades. Everything north of the town nucleus was the Jades, and oh, how the money rolled in! In spite of the financial crisis. Farming, oil, textiles, they did it. Anything south though was for the Sleuths. All of it was good too ... fine land ... and it stretched far on both sides of the train line. But even though the Jades were making money, there still was an inherent problem for them.

"See, as far as the rail cars and tracks, the advantage was with the Sleuths, because of the side their land was on. They were reaping the benefits of being able to ship extra cargo into Houston and out of the shores of Galveston. As well as having that extension going into Gheldoux. And that's how they sustained and built more wealth through that rough decade. The Jades wanted to, but couldn't go further north, because it was too far from the infrastructure they needed. They thought of other building strategies for a time, like extending the rail line in other directions and all that, but it just never took. Once you head away from the main line, you head away from the supply line — the Jades needed it, and the Sleuths had it."

Poppy paused to take another sip of coffee. Over his cup, his eyes flashed excitedly at Libby.

"So, what happened?" Libby asked. It was clearly the right question, because Poppy shifted in his seat and started to rub his hands together in circles.

"Well," he started again, "That's the sixty-four-million-dollar question. See, things actually started changing in '28, before the Depression. First the patriarch of the Sleuth family, name of Judah Edgar, died suddenly. Very healthy man too, but he was gone quick. So his son took over. Fine young man by the name of Irving, but within a year he was dead. Accident in his car, one of the back roads here.

"Then his brother Michael came on. Not such a fine young man — a drinker and gambler. But still, he understood family business and he did it alright, before he vanished."

"Vanished?" said Libby frowning.

"Yup, there one minute, gone the next," Poppy explained. "No trace. They thought he'd caught some bad business down in Houston."

Libby's eyes widened, and she quietly said, "I see."

"Well, by now the Sleuth family was getting worried about still having suitable relatives around, cause many of them had left to find and add to their fortune elsewhere," Poppy went on. "The Jades knew this, and were sniffing around the land holdings. But then a spritely young woman, a niece of Judah's, took up the reins. Her name was Teresa. Married to a Klein fella. She did good, very good. Ran the business into a winning! Money came in and the family looked like it was back on track. But just like that," Poppy clapped his hand once before finishing, "she was dead. Straight up poisoned. Black tongue, purple mouth. It's one of the oldest stories in the town. Happened at the ball!"

Here Poppy paused and watched Libby, as they both took a long sip of their coffees. When she said nothing more, he continued.

"Now Teresa's daughter, Lilly Klein ... well by then she was married, so her name was Peck ... she swore that the family misfortune was the doing of the Jades. Swore that the Jades wanted all the land, and all the oil. Money does strange things to people, and Lilly was a firecracker like her mother. By now the war had started, and business was up and down. The Sleuths managed to get a contract with the military, and used the rail lines to transport equipment into the city. This gave them more big money. Lilly was at the helm with her husband, Jeffrey Peck, and again the family looked good.

"But then the men here had to go off to war, and even though he was older than the normal recruit, Jeffrey was one of them. And he never came back. Other Sleuth men, living in other places at the time, also went to war and unfortunately, did not make it back either. The ones that managed to make it back, they had other investments. This is starting to be established money now, remember — not just in this town but other places too. That left Lilly Peck still running the business in Atheneum. But then she went missing too. Went swimming and was never seen again.

"Well, by now things should be looking very suspicious, right? You'd think that someone would take charge of looking into the cases of the unfortunate Sleuths, because the family was in trouble. The only close relative was George Sleuth. He was the great-great nephew of Judah Sleuth, offspring of one of his older brothers. He was a college professor in Dallas. Professor of Philosophy no less. Other than him, there was only Lilly's daughter Miriam, who was ten when Jeffrey met his fate in the war.

"George took over, but he had no interest or knowledge of the land or how to use it. He tried it for a few years, but he wanted a quiet life without the hassle. So, he sold it in 1948. To the Jades of course, for pittance. All except for one large spit of land. Powerful land, very much also wanted by the Jade family. There was a certain symbolism and cachet to it, as it was the land that Lorenzo Athens had acquired when he graced the town. But in his line of business, my personal belief was that he bought, or just plain took over land in so many places, that it was hard to keep up with it all. Or maybe he just didn't care about it, because he never came back here after he established the railroad. And since it's on the outskirts of town, going into Gheldoux, the Sleuths just quietly took it over unnoticed when the Threadgoods were leaving.

"This special piece, George left to Miriam, and then he took her with him away from the town. It wouldn't have been hard to find them if the Jades wanted them completely gone, but I don't think that they wanted to rock the boat at the time after all of the other 'circumstances.'

"So the land sat there, and the Jades wanted it, wanted it bad. But they had to leave it alone for the time being. Prime real estate at that, near the rail, close to the oil, fit for mining, sittin' there, driving the Jades close to madness. But no Sleuths left to," Poppy formed air quotes and finished with, "make disappear or buy it from."

Poppy sat back, eyes flashing with a smirk on his face. He looked happy with his story.

"So then ... the Jades were left here, practically all alone after all that? Never investigated?" Libby asked.

"Investigated for what?" Poppy replied. "No evidence, no trace of the missing, no foul play that would ever be proved. They stayed, and they took over the town. Fingers into every pie. Kept the scent off of Miriam's land. Every law-man, politician, and real estate magnate there is — is in the pockets of the Jades. All the way from here to Gheldoux, and parts of north Houston. They say wear red, you wear red. And if you don't wear red, they got all the power in the world to make Atheneum, and every darn place near it difficult for you. Everyone knows that the Jades make the rules, and people like me remember some of the Sleuths and how they disappeared."

Poppy fell silent and drank the last of his coffee, and Libby too sat contemplating and mesmerized by the book before her.

"And all that's in this book here?" she asked.

"That's why it's Reference," Poppy replied. "It has a way of never being returned if it's left for check out. It's a good thing that there is no way to get it past the RFID scanners without it beeping. I'm glad that those are there."

"So the land?" Libby shook her head "what of it now?"

"Ahhh." Poppy once again rubbed his hands together. "Yessss. See Miriam went away, and by all rumors and accounts, she lived a very colorful, but not necessarily righteous life right up into her eighties. But now she has passed and the land, worth millions, is left."

"Left? That seems unbelievable after all of these years. The Jades sound very ambitious and greedy, and it's weird that they did not pursue taking over the land since the forties."

"Yup, she left a will, and in it she left the land to a rightful heir of the Sleuth slash Klein fortune. And interested parties know the name of the heir. But that is being kept quiet amongst old rumors. See, when she left Atheneum, Miriam was 'in a family way,' and the offspring was rumored to be that of Charles Brandon Jade."

Libby's eyebrows rose, and a little smile crept over her face.

"Yes, saucy isn't it?" said Poppy with a happy glint in his eyes. He clearly loved the town's dirty laundry. "So when Miriam Peck left this virtual fortune to an heir that has not shown their face, it tipped the balance that the Jade family had on this town. See, in all the years since Miriam and George left, the Jades, they had control of who came and went. If there was an investor from one of those big corporations that so much as sniffed in the direction of Atheneum, the Jades saw to it that they were gone as quick as they came. And this started happening without any new mysterious disappearances and accidents.

"So let's just say that if you feel a little bite to the town, you're not the only one. The Jades and the whole town, who are related to them in one way or another by blood or by money, have been pushing outsiders out of this place for years. Someone so much as thinks about buying a drink in this town better get the approval of the Jade empire before he does it."

"So this is about a piece of land then?" asked Libby.

"Yes and no," Poppy answered. "It's about the land, yes, definitely. The executor of the will needs to find the heir. George never married, and so Miriam's heir or heirs are the last left that can claim this land. Well, as far as anyone can tell.

"But if they can't be found, the land will go to the state," Poppy concluded. "And who do you think has a finger in that pie?"

"The Jades," said Libby just above a whisper.

"Yup. Brandon Jade is waiting," Poppy added. He's the main investor of the family, you know? He's the tycoon land owner of the lot, even at his young age. But I think that's more or less that some of the older family members were just ready to give up some of the responsibility. Others just want to see what he is made of, and what ability he has of amassing more prestige and prosperity for the Jades.

"He's waiting for that land to become state-owned," Poppy said, and then looked directly at Libby with intensity. He then asked, "With no heir and no other investors, who do you think is a shoo-in for that property?"

Libby left the questioned unanswered. She knew, of course. If the Jade family was the powerhouse behind Atheneum, and the town was all related to them in one way or another, as Poppy had said, then it wasn't necessarily personal. It wasn't great, to be sure, but it wasn't Libby who they disliked particularly. It was a general distrust of everyone, for many years at that. It explained the town's coolness.

Something nagged at Libby though, and she wanted to say something to Poppy about it, but there was a familiar voice that called over to them.

"Poppy!" Ruthie appeared by their table.

"Hi, Ruthie!" said Libby, her mind reaching back to the dreams she'd had. She was relieved to see the girl looking well.

"Hi!" waved Ruthie, but hurried on with what she had to say. "Poppy. Mommy's in the car and she says to tell you she's double-parked, and that she can't come in, and you have to come right now."

Ruthie looked pleased to have delivered her message without error and beamed from ear to ear.

Poppy laughed and said "Well, I guess that's all the time I have today. It has been a pleasure to have your company for this short spell, Miss Libby."

He rose slowly to his feet, Ruthie's hand grabbing his. Libby rose too.

"You enjoy that book while you're here," said Poppy, and he gave Libby a quick wink.

Libby smiled back and watched them turn to leave. Poppy leaned down to tell Ruthie something that made her giggle and squirm. Libby glanced down at the book on the table. It was opened to the 'About the Author' page. Staring back at her was a man in his mid-fifties with gray hair and a familiar twinkle in his eye.

Libby was momentarily surprised. "Poppy," she called. "Did you write this?" She held up the book as he turned to her. "Did you write this book? Are you Dr. Grant T. Uldrich?"

Poppy chuckled and winked again, and Libby pointed at his photograph.

"This is you!" she said.

"I know," he said and turned again to walk away.

Libby let him get to the door, and a nagging feeling made her call to him again.

"Poppy," she said, and he turned around again.

"Uhhh ...," she paused, and then just waved and said, "Bye."

He gave her a questioning look before he resumed his stroll out of the door. She had been about to tell him that Sleuth was her family name.

But not even she was supposed to know that.

Chapter Six
by Stephanie Adams

Libby unceremoniously packed clothes and toiletries into a suitcase. She barely concentrated on what she was packing. It wasn't yet five a.m., but she rushed because she just wanted to get out of the house as fast as possible. She told herself that she would be back in the cottage once she made amends with her family and came back to Texas to get her belongings. Right now, she just wanted to get on the road.

As she put her suitcase into the trunk of her car, thoughts and questions filled her mind. *Who did Brandon think he was? How dare he speak about my work performance, or lack thereof? He does not even work at HouBayou.*

Libby was so frustrated by the antics at work. It had been a great opportunity, but at what cost? She was so unhappy there. And last night was the last straw.

Jane had pointed out to Libby that no one was really being mean to her at the workplace. But someone *was* mistreating her, and he did not even work there. Why is the company letting an outsider bother her? Just because his brother Wilson works there, Brandon is still an outsider, and Libby has no one to complain to. There's no actual Human Resources department to bridge communication gaps between company management and employees, and offer an opportunity to release her frustrations with the company and report wrongdoings. Libby has not seen any plan of HouBayou effectively communicating and listening to employee concerns. Their payroll, benefits, and additional compensations are outsourced to an independent company.

During the event celebrating renowned author Nora Grisham Patterson's twentieth book of one of her very popular series published by HouBayou, Brandon loudly pointed out that Libby had not posted any acclamations about the new release on the media page before her long weekend.

Within earshot of Angela Lamar and other coworkers he then questioned, "Did you really need extra time off after *not* working hard last week?"

Libby was too stunned to speak. Then she was tempted to throw her cup of punch in his face, but he was standing too far away. There were reasons and excuses that had started to formulate in her head, but she just couldn't get any of them out.

She blames Wilson for allowing Brandon to hang around the office likes he's some important person, but there are other people there that should put a stop to it. Brandon is so irrelevant to anything that happens in the building. What does he know about books? He is into real estate. And with the things that he talks and brags about, he also seems to be into swindling.

After merging off of I-45, she drove east on I-10 toward Louisiana. She tried to listen to an audiobook that she had downloaded to her cell phone from the library's website, but she could not focus on the story. After Poppy had left on Monday, she had learned from Daisy the different apps available for downloading and viewing e-books and magazines, as well as audiobook and movie streaming that was free through the library. She immediately made a digital checkout of an Edgar Allan Poe thriller, with plans to start listening to audiobooks on her walks. Right now, though, her mind kept drifting away from the narration, and stubbornly traveling back to the night before. This kept her simmering in anger.

She opted for the radio instead, and kept it there until the stations that she was familiar with began to fade out and get staticky. The last song she heard clearly was a new one by Oow Oow E$$ence on 93.7, and after that, there was nothing but static on all of her presets. She had reached Winnie by that point. She had an hour and thirty minutes left to drive before she got to her childhood home in Lacassine.

Libby then switched to satellite radio, deciding to listen to clips of stand-up comedians. Her favorite channel was the Ridiculous Relatives station. She hoped that it would lighten her mood, which was probably be a good idea since she was on her way to see her family. After two years of not seeing her parents, she did not know what to expect. She did not even know if they would be home at this time on a Wednesday. It was still pretty early though, and she might be able to catch them before leaving for work.

Once she got to Lake Charles, Libby stopped at the Claim Jumper Restaurant on Golden Nugget Boulevard for a quick bite. She had eaten here with her family numerous times growing up. She thought that some nostalgia and some comforting pancakes would be a good idea. She was too nervous to eat much, so she only ordered a short stack of two, and also had coffee.

Once fueled and caffeinated, Libby completed her trip to see her parents. At the house, she pulled into the massive driveway, and only saw one car parked there. But she knew that others could be in the multiple-car garage.

She sat in her car and looked at the beige stucco on the exterior of the house. She studied the unique combination of curves and geometric shapes. Every line was clean and straight, with the rest of the color scheme in walnut and chiffon. There were multiple slopes and pitches to the roof over the many rooms of the house.

The windows took up entire walls with polished steel beams that broke them into more rectangles. The enormity of them had sometimes scared her when she was little. There were cedar beams on the porch, with raised plant beds that contained Bells of Ireland flowers and numerous ferns.

Once she had built up the slightest modicum of courage, she ascended the wide steps, and rang the doorbell. It didn't take long for her brother to answer the door. He seemed happy to see her. Almost too happy. He hugged her immediately in the doorway, and kept her in a tight embrace for at least thirty seconds. This grasp made her start crying right away. She had missed him a lot. He let her go momentarily before squeezing her tight again.

Her brother was two years younger than Libby, and was her only sibling. If his studies were going according to plan, he would be entering Johns Hopkins for medical school this fall.

"My goodness, Richie," she said, using his nickname as she tried to catch her breath. "You're going to squeeze the life out of me."

He was the only family member that she had spoken to in the two years that she had been gone. Libby had called the family's landline a few times and left voicemails for her parents, but her calls were not returned. Her parents also did not answer when she called their cell phones.

But Richard happily answered her calls on his cell phone, and they talked quite a few times during the first year that she was gone.

And then he changed his number.

Beyond the foyer, the bottom floor of the lavish home had a large, open plan, and there was a floating stairway leading to the upper floors. Libby looked up and saw her mother standing at the overlook with a scowl on her face. Richard closed the door, and he and Libby walked into the living room.

"Hey Nathaniel. Come see this," her mother bellowed toward her parents' bedroom. "Just look at this."

Her mother waited there until Libby's father came out, and then they descended the stairs together into the living room. Her father had an ambiguous look on his face. He did not look surprised, happy, or angry. He just looked plain.

"What are you doing here *now*?" her mother asked. She kept standing while Libby's father sat down on one of their expensive, imported couches. Richard walked to a corner of the room and took his cell phone out of the front pocket of his designer jeans.

Two years of pent-up rage is what must have made her mother not wait for an answer. She went into a full attack and started yelling at Libby.

"We paid your college tuition and expenses for four years and made sure that you didn't have to work during that time!" Her whole face was saturated in fury as she continued. "We foolishly sat here and thought that you were on a pre-med track to become a doctor and join our family practice!"

Libby loudly and tearfully retorted, as she had never really stopped crying since Nathaniel, Jr. hugged her. "I never once said anything about being a doctor! That was your assumption! You could have seen the courses that I was taking, but you never asked! You never cared what I was doing!

"Oh, no Missy! We always cared!" Her mother lowered her voice and stepped closer to Libby. "Long before you ever went to college ... oh yes we did. Every important society function and event that happened around Lake Charles or Lacassine, we made sure we were a part of it. Yet here you were, resisting them as much as you could. We practically had to drag you to each affair to hobnob with the elite!

"All you ever wanted to do was go to the library and come home with tons of books about other people's lives, waiting and expecting some happy ending," her mother huffed and threw back her head slightly. In a snarky tone she added, "Days full of roses, and nights full of starlight touching snow. That's just all fantasy and delusion. That's not the real world!"

Libby knew that if her parents were so confident in her joining the family practice, they would have been on top of the situation throughout her undergraduate years. It would have been a constant topic of conversation. If they thought that she was going to continue on to medical school, they would have known which ones she had applied to or chosen. She and her parents would have been able to relate to each other, and might have bonded through the situation. The two of them would have told her stories and used examples about experiencing the same thing that she was going through at the time.

Libby's emotions and thoughts were in a disarray. She wiped her tears with the palm of her left hand. In the two years that she had been gone, she always knew the likelihood that this current scene was going to be the result of her homecoming. However, she was thrown off by the fact that she was being berated for her past of spending time at the library and wanting to read books. She did not know how to defend herself against that, and her mother's continued tirade barely gave her the chance to even think of one.

"You probably didn't wanna become a doctor because you didn't want to get your precious hands dirty," her mother persisted. Even though you could have gained great prestige, you didn't want the hard work that goes into it."

"Dirty is a subjective term when it comes to you," Libby said.

"What's that supposed to mean?"

"Oh. You know exactly what I mean," Libby's voice was barely above a whisper.

This silenced her mother. She stood in front of Libby, her chest rising and falling in rapid heaves. Her father had yet to speak, but at this, he grabbed a velvet pillow from the couch and used both hands to squeeze the sides of it.

Her mother walked to the large front windows. "I see you are still driving the Maserati that we bought you for your college graduation," she said after peering out. "Before that, you spent your other years of college in the BMW that we bought you for your high school graduation.

"We even surprised you with it at the beginning of your last semester. We decided to go against the cliché of waiting until you walked across the stage." She turned back around to look at Libby. "Which you didn't even bother to do."

Libby looked over at her brother. He lowered his head.

"What's wrong? Whatever crappy job you got, is it not paying you enough?" her mother asked. "Or do you even have a job? You never did answer my question as to why you are here. Back to grovel for forgiveness? Or a handout?"

Her family didn't know it, of course, but Libby used a meager amount of her HouBayou income to pay for rent, water, and electricity in the small cottage. Her mother would probably faint if she saw the small quarters that Libby lived in. Based on the palatial domicile that she came from, her mother would think that cottage would only be fit for a pauper.

But it suits Libby's needs, and other expenses are practically nonexistent. She has no children, and definitely has no friends. Therefore, there is no hanging out in any type of form. Fine dining is non-existent. She likes the taste of home-cooked meals over take-out, so she cooks breakfast and dinner at home, and packs her lunch for work. Since HouBayou is in Atheneum, she also does not spend much on fueling her car.

Her mother stepped back into her face again. "You always thought that you were better than us."

"I am us!" Libby screamed. She felt as if she had been slapped.

Her mother's face reddened, and she opened her mouth to speak or yell again. But Libby's father got up from the couch and pulled her mother away before she got any words out.

"I think that your mom is a little taken aback from the surprise of you being here," he said. "This might not be the best time for a visit. Just go back to your hotel for now. We need time to regroup."

This was all avoidance jargon. Visit? Regroup? They had no way of knowing that Libby was there to explore the idea of moving back home. But her father's statement, along with her mother's chiding made it strikingly clear that it was not something that either of them would consider.

All along, maybe they had been relieved when she did not return home after college. 'Good riddance to bad rubbish' may have been in their thoughts for the past two years. All she knew was that right now, they were not happy to see her.

Although she did show up unannounced, if they loved her at all, they would have been at least somewhat thrilled to see her and would have tried to find out the real purpose of her visit. Besides the accusations from her mother, not once did anyone ask about her life for the past two years. She was their daughter for goodness sakes, yet they were showing that they cared nothing about her.

Her father moved to the front door and opened it for Libby to exit. She took one last look at both her mother and her brother before she slowly walked out.

On the other side of the threshold, she turned and faced the house before her father softly closed the door. She decided not to let them continue to look at the sorrow on her face through the door glass, so she turned around to the street. She wiped her face again with her palm and took a few deep breaths. She swiped her hand hard against a fern to knock it off the ledge, and make sure that its pot broke on the porch.

She got into her car and started it. She closed her eyes and breathed deeply for a full minute. Once she felt calm enough, she opened her eyes and put the car in reverse. Without checking her mirrors, she began backing up, but stopped when she heard someone yelling.

All of a sudden, her cousin appeared at the window next to her. She pressed the button to roll it down.

"Wow, Libs. You almost took me out," he said jovially. "Where are you going in such a hurry? Richie texted me and said that you just got here."

It was her cousin Jacob, who lived in Lake Charles. Although he sounded as though he was happy to have come over to see her, she just could not deal with any more family right then.

"I'm sorry Jacob," she said. "I just gotta go. I'll see you some other time."

And with that, Libby swiftly receded out of the driveway, and started her drive back to Texas.

Chapter Seven
by Maria Christina Yardas

Libby pulled into her driveway, alongside another car parked there. She then saw Angela standing in front of her house. Angela approached her as she got out of the car.

"Here you are, thank goodness!" Angela said, and hugged Libby.

Libby stiffened, and kept her arms at her sides.

"When you didn't show up to work and didn't call, I got so worried," she exclaimed, and let go of Libby.

Libby looked at Angela as though she had three heads.

Angela noticed this and said, "I know. I know." She put her hands on her temples and moved them to the crown of her head before dropping them.

"First let me start by apologizing to you," she went on. "What Brandon said to you last night was out of line. I am so sorry that he did that."

Libby still kept looking at her in the same way.

"Trust me," Angela continued. "Brandon gets on my nerves, too. I wish that he wasn't always coming by to see Wilson. But our hands are tied. There's nothing that any of us there can do about it."

That didn't make sense to Libby, so she asked, "Why not? Aren't you and William the ones in charge?"

"Yes," Angela answered. "But it does go deeper than that. And simply, if we ban one employee from having family members there, then we have to ban all employees from having family members there. It won't be pleasant for our business environment."

And just like that, with the first part of Angela's statement, things were clearer to Libby. There always seemed to be invisible strings pulling things around the company. But she wasn't going to agree or acknowledge it out loud.

"And there is one thing that I learned years ago about them Jades," Angela started walking away, and didn't bother to turn around before she finished the last part of her statement. "If you can't beat 'em, join 'em."

She was almost to her car, but she returned to Libby. "One more thing. I know that tomorrow is your birthday, so you don't have to come in if you don't want to. Go do something fun for the day. We'll see you Friday." She walked back to her car and left.

Libby had practically forgotten that tomorrow was her 25th birthday. But now that Angela brought it up, there was no doubt that her mind would stay on it now.

She was tired from her fast trip to Lacassine and back. She went into the house, changed into something comfortable, and got right into bed. She quickly drifted off to sleep.

***

Libby woke up around five that evening and laid in bed thinking for another hour. She tried to remember and figure out if she ever really had any dreams, and tried to realize what her life purpose was now? She wondered, "Am I a strong person that was ready to face the world?" She was at the age where that would be important and expected.

Libby thought of herself as a sweet person, with a strong personality, that which had been muted in the past three years. There were occasions in the past when people seemed to take advantage of her, or dismiss her feelings. This occurred within her family, more often than outside of it. This made her feel weak at times, and gave her moments of low self-esteem. People think she's half-Asian blood because of her sleek, raven hair, and her tiny eyes. She has a pale skin color, and low dimples on the side of her cheeks that make her prettier when she smiles.

    While Libby is pondering what her life should be, and where it is going, she decides to take Angela's advice. But instead of waiting until tomorrow, she decided to have fun tonight at a place that would be expected to lift her spirits.

    She had heard people at work talking about a local place called Gerry's, and from those conversations, she knows it is just the type of business for just what she is seeking right now. On top of that, it is not a far walk from her house. Libby got out of bed and prepared to leave to get something soothing.

    It was only about 7 pm, and the establishment did not have many customers there. Libby thought maybe that was because it was still early, although she did not even know what a normal amount of people would be for the place. She picked a dark corner and hoped to be inconspicuous.

    She saw a double-dispensing device beyond the main counter. Both sides were mixing up something slushy inside, with one side a mint color, and the other one peach. When her server came over, she ordered a large green one.

Libby pulled out her phone and started playing some of her word games. She slurped the beverage astonishingly quick, and ordered another one of the same size. She continued playing games on her phone, and also went to her Facebook page. As she had done numerous times in the past year, after he had changed his phone number, she searched for her brother's name.

As usual, there was no account for him. He and her parents were staying true to what they said years ago – that they had no interest in that type of social media.

Libby looked up to find her server, and thought she saw a man staring at her from a darkened hallway. She thought she had noticed it earlier too. She tried to make out who he was, but she felt a little light-headed and dizzy, like there was a delayed brain freeze from the frosty beverages.

Her waiter came over and asked if she was okay. As he had done earlier, he once again told her the specials, and asked her if she wanted to order any food.

Her words were choppy, and she was a little loud when she held up her plastic cup and said, "Just one more of these please! Tomorrow's my birthday!"

This visit to Gerry's was out of Libby's normal routine, and the effects were becoming evident. She got up to go the restroom. She pushed open the first door that she saw in the hallway under the signs.

"You need to get out of here, or you're going to mess everything up! And then Melly's going to be—," Libby heard a familiar raspy voice as she noticed urinals along the wall.

"Hey, this is the men's room," a tall, well-toned man said while quickly grabbing her to lead her out. She managed to get a quick look at the other, much older man in the restroom. "Pah … pah" was all that she managed to get out before the man holding her guided her, and pretty much shoved her into the ladies' room.

Once she left the restroom and started approaching her table, she thought she must have been going to the wrong one, because sitting there was her cousin Jacob. She also thought that he had been the one that grabbed her out of the men's room. She had been a little jingled in those moments, and she had not been sure what she was seeing.

The last green slushie that she had ordered was there on the table. Libby sat down, took a big gulp, and started coughing.

"Whoa there, Libs," Jacob said, and softly patted her back. "Slow down. You know that you can't drink icy beverages that fast. That brain freeze has a way of sneaking up on you, and stopping you in your tracks. Maybe I should finish this one for you."

"No. Get your own." She called out, "Waiter. Waiter!"

With an annoyed look, her server came over. "Yes, Miss?"

"We'll just take the check," Jacob said before Libby could order anything else.

The server's face formed with concern as he looked at Libby. He opened his mouth to say something, and although Libby didn't know what it was going to be, she said, "I'm good. I can go home."

Libby closed her eyes and started humming.

"What song is that, Libby?" Jacob asked.

"'Home on the Range,' Cuz," she answered. "And you know I sound good."

Libby continued her humming. Her cousin told the waiter, "Don't worry. I will assist her."

The waiter looked at Jacob and was still a little hesitant before reaching into his stiff, black booklet. He finally did, and placed Libby's check onto the table.

Jacob winked at him.

***

"Don't fight. Please-please don't fight," Libby said.

She tried to walk on her skis to get to the women, but her left foot accidentally stepped on the ski attached to her right foot. When she tried to take the next step, she went face down into the snow. She rolled onto her back, and then positioned herself to get back up. She sat upright and put her left hand on the ground to get ready to push off and propel her body upward.

But before she could do that, she saw a gleaming item, and heard a loud bang.

Although they were open, her eyes were bleary, and she mildly started to panic when she noticed an indistinct man sitting in an armchair on the other side of the room.

"You slept so good," he said. "Until these last few minutes."

She lay immobilized, and there was fear in her voice. "Why am I here? Where did you bring me?" The identity of the man was apparently of less importance in her questioning.

The man started laughing, and that made her notice the throbbing in her head. She rubbed her forehead, before moving her fingers to her eyes.

"I made you some breakfast soup to help you feel better," the man said.

Without seeing him, that's when she realized that the man was Jacob. She had yet to meet anyone else that liked having soup for breakfast.

She stopped rubbing and opened her eyes. She saw that she was on her own couch.

"I tried to be as quiet as I could while you were sleeping," Jacob said, and got up to go to the kitchen. It was an open-concept design with the living room area, and he was able to continue his conversation with Libby.

"I like how your fridge was already stocked with great items that I could use," he informed her. "I didn't even have to drive around to find a store."

"Yeah. Wonderful. It smells great," Libby said with a sharp edge to each word. His face turned to hurt as she peered at him.

She softened her tone. "What are you doing in Atheneum? How did you find me?"

"I followed you from Lacassine," he explained. "I haven't seen you since you disappeared from college two years ago. Then you show up at your parent's house, and just leave again in a flash. I couldn't let you get away again. I've been worried about you.

She disregarded his explanation and continued to study him. He looked away uncomfortably and began looking in her cabinets.

"Were you talking to an old man in the bathroom at Gerry's last night?" Libby asked. "It looked like someone that I recently met and talked to about some — history."

Jacob placed two bowls on the small dividing island and didn't answer. When he looked over and saw Libby glowering at him, he let out a small laugh. "Oh. You were serious?" he chortled.

He paused to wait for an answer. When one didn't come he said, "Ummm ... First of all ... I wouldn't hold a conversation with anyone in a bathroom. Not even in my own house.

"Secondly, how would you have seen me in the bathroom there? You know that most places supply men and women with their own separate facilities, right?" Jacob laughed.

When Libby still did not respond, Jacob upturned his hands, hunched his shoulders, and gave her a questioning look.

"Never mind," she said, but didn't take her eyes off his face.

She waited several seconds before continuing the conversation. "So what's Aunt Melanie been up to?"

"Who's that?"

"Your mom."

"Libby. What on Earth are you talking about? You know my mother's name is Jean."

Libby still stared at Jacob. She finally said, "Oh, that's right. What am I saying?" Libby took a deep breath. "I don't know. My head hurts, and I think that I am delirious from the nightmare that I just had. I'm mixing people up."

"Yeahhhh," Jacob dragged. "I'm *sure* that's it. Nothing else from last night."

"That's my story, and I'm," Libby stopped, and started rubbing her temples.

Jacob inquired, "So you were having a nightmare? I thought so by the way you started thrashing around a few minutes before you woke up."

"Yeah. I was. But I don't want to talk about it."

"We can definitely change the subject. Because I'd rather know what happened two years ago."

Libby huffed. "What do you mean? Nothing happened."

"That's ludicrous! Something definitely happened!" Jacob went straight to yelling. "No one just leaves college in their graduating semester and disappears from their family!"

Libby was not expecting this, and barely stammered out, "I, I ... just ... needed to get away! Get off my back!"

"No. No way." Jacob spoke and shook his head while walking toward Libby. "I have tried to make sense of it all this time, and now that I finally have you in front of me, we are going to talk about it!"

Libby leaped off the couch. "Jacob, get out!" She pointed a hand toward the door, but then grabbed her head in an attempt to thwart off an increase to the excruciating pain that she had already been feeling.

"Look at what you are doing to me! After all of this time, why must you still torment me?" she asked.

Jacob retreated back into the kitchen with his hands up in defeat. He remained that way until Libby looked a little calmer.

When she lowered her hands, and her face softened, he said, "You're absolutely right. I did pester you a lot while we were growing up. And your brother, too.

"I was overweight as a child, and schoolmates picked on me for that. I was supposed to be two grades ahead of you, but I got 'left back' one year. I was called bad names and picked on for both of those things. And yes — I did take that out on you."

Jacob lowered his head in shame and exhaled. "I have since learned that people often hurt those that are closest to them. My mother had no mate and was raising me on her own. She was always at the hospital, working long shifts as a registered nurse, and also still taking more schooling to earn a doctorate. I was staying with your family all the time. You and Richie were right there, and I took the pain that I was feeling out on the two of you.

"And *you* always persevered," Jacob said, took a hard look at Libby, and pounded his closed fist on the counter. "Not just from my anguish and torture, but even in your own physical pain. You were getting major headaches all the time and were absent from school all the time. Yet you never failed. Always kept up your schoolwork. Never got held back like me.

"Ugh! That made me so mad!" He opened and slammed shut a cabinet door.

Libby was immediately stuck on one thing and asked about that. "Headaches. What headaches?"

Jacob's chest heaved rapidly. "Oh, you got headaches all the time, and we had to be so quiet and careful around you all the time. That wasn't cool. Already I had to stay at someone else's house. Couldn't be at my own. And then on top of that I couldn't make a peep?"

Jacob opened and slammed shut the same cabinet door in rapid succession. "Couldn't disturb the precious Libby!"

Jacob turned his head to look at her, and Libby sensed that he noticed her dumbfounded expression.

"What? You don't remember all of the pampering you got?" he asked.

Libby still had a puzzled expression on her face.

"Maybe not." He let go off the knob on the cabinet and ran his hands through dark brown hair. "I think you outgrew those headaches before you even hit middle school," he said.

Although she had no recollection of the headaches that Jacob was speaking of, she figured that he was most likely not making them up. Libby immediately started to wonder if those were related to the nightmares of the present. She sat back down on the couch to think, but Jacob's rant kept her from being able to start contemplating further.

"You were planning to go to college, so I decided to get my act together and to go to college," Jacob barely stopped to take a breath. "There was a year between mine and your high school graduations. During that time, I applied to the same colleges that you applied. I got accepted and enrolled at the same place that you decided to enroll.

"And I barely left your side the whole four years. I was your protector. I made sure that no one took advantage of you anymore during those years."

"Yeah. That was great," Libby whispered. "Just a different way of bullying and tormenting me."

Jacob did not appear to hear her, and he kept talking.

"We made it all the way to our senior year. I was so proud of myself. I thought, Hey. Despite my inferior upbringing in comparison to yours, I was now on an even-keel with you. Even more so, especially since I was planning to go into medicine, like my mom, and your parents. Instead of your crazy 'Literature' major.

"Then, that Fall, you had some big genealogy project to do for one of your History classes. You were at the library for hours, using their free Ancestry and Heritage Quest databases to research and find what you could on your Ferguson ancestors. We went home during Thanksgiving break, and you asked your parents some questions about your family history. They told you that they never heard much from their parents and grandparents about that type of thing, and there wasn't anything that they knew.

"But you did not want to take that for an answer," Jacob now mentioning things that Libby already knew. "You snooped in their file cabinets and photo albums, and questioned them about some of your findings online at the library.

"They were not happy about that. They told me not to let you turn in your assignment. Like I had any control over that. What was I going to do? Tackle you at the classroom door that day? I just stood back, and let the pieces fall where they may."

"Wait," Libby said. "Let the pieces fall where they may? You mean you already knew that something wasn't on the up and up in our family?"

"No!" Jacob raised his voice. "That is not what I said. No!"

Jacob paced the floor. "I shouldn't have even brought that project up." He closed his eyes and took some deep breaths.

"What I meant to say was, all of a sudden, in the Spring semester, you just disappeared one day," he reasoned. "Moved out of your dorm without a trace. I called your parents, and they said that you had not come home. They dismissed my concerns by saying that you probably had some mid-term exam that you might have been stressing about, and you would probably turn up in 'a couple of days.'

"But you didn't. You have been gone, and I have been worried about you ever since."
Jacob came and sat down on the couch with Libby.

A few minutes passed before Libby spoke. "Well, that was a lot to be said. I'm glad to know that you were worried about me all of this time," her voice was shaky, and sounded like she was about to start crying. "My visit to Lacassine yesterday showed me that my parents definitely have not been worried or concerned about my whereabouts at all."

Jacob put one of her hands in his. Libby cleared her throat and said, "I know that you know this by now, especially since you were the one that bullied me into investing with your friend."

Jacob laughed. "You are really taking that 'bully' word and running with it."

That confirmed with Libby that Jacob had heard her before.

She gave a small chuckle. "Anyway. Your friend came to me and told me that I had made a mint on my investment. So I took the money and ran."

"Wait, what?" Jacob asked. "That's why you disappeared?"

"Yeah," she responded. "I was stinking rich. So I left school."

Jacob cleared his throat and rubbed his eyes. "Libby?"

"What?"

"You know that's crazy, right?"

"Nooooo ..." Libby dragged out the word and looked at Jacob as though he had just grown another head. "What's crazy about getting rich?"

Jacob cocked his head to the side, and patted Libby's hand. "You left school like a month after I told you to invest the money. Even though the crypto game is pretty stupendous for some people, a big return investment doesn't usually happen that fast."

"But it was your friend that said—" Libby snatched her hand from his and jumped up off the couch. "Are you telling me that that was also a fraud? There's no money?"

"I'm not saying that there isn't any money. I'm just saying that it is unbelievable that it was that quick," Jacob said. "You haven't cashed it in or whatever?"

Libby spoke rapidly, "What about you? Did you make any money from him?"

"I didn't have anything to invest. There was no 'Mommy Daddy' money like you had to just hand over to him," Jacob scoffed.

"But what do you mean, also a fraud?" he asked. "If you haven't even tried to get the money, then how can you think—"

"Nothing. Never mind. I was thinking of something else," Libby said in exasperation. She bolted for the front door. "It's just that my head hurts. I've got to get some air."

She ran to the front gate and intended to go out and start walking. Jacob had just hit her with some heavy stuff, and she needed to think and rationalize those things through.

But Libby stopped suddenly right after opening the gate. A man and a little girl were just walking past, both eating ice cream cones, and

Libby had not even noticed them while she was running to get away.

It immediately reminded her of the times her father would pick her up after school, and they would go to Shamrock Ice Cream Shoppe in Lacassine. The establishment was set up to be reminiscent of soda fountain counters that were commonly found in pharmacies in the fifties. Libby didn't know about the historical aspect then. She just liked being there with her dad, spending time together, and eating special treats. She remembered that her favorite there was the coconut strawberry ice cream, and her dad always got the pistachio flavor. Once Richard started school, he would go with them also, and it was even more fun then.

She missed her dad so much. She had a lot of memories of being with him more than her mom. She remembered their weekend mornings of going biking, and playing volleyball at the park, as well as time together watching her favorite Disney movies, and going shopping at the mall.

"Why did you turn me away yesterday?" Libby said.

The man and girl turned around to look at her. "Pardon?" he asked.

But Libby didn't hear him.

"Don't fight. Please-please don't fight," Libby said.

Libby tried to walk down the aisle of the plane to get to her mother and aunt, but the turbulence was making the plane shift about. She fell on the floor, and another big wind gust made her roll sideways until her head hit the metal on the bottom of a seat. There was intense pain from that, but she managed to get up on all fours.

When she looked down the aisle, she saw something shiny, but all she could hear were whooshes from the air pockets outside.

Chapter Eight
by Osiria Kage

The train was consistent.

It came three times each day: once just after Libby's morning walk, once at noon even, and once in the dead of night. Most nights it was just background noise for the landscape of her dreamless sleep, and if the horn woke her up, it was easy for her to return to sleep. She counted facts, things she knew were certain, until sleep's comforting darkness came to embrace her again.

That night, Libby slipped in and out of the claws of tumultuous nightmares. They were always the same, the location ever changing, the women fighting, the echoing *bang*, and the name. Melanie.

Libby knew that name. Jacob insisted his mother's name was Jean, but Libby's entire being screamed otherwise. Nothing seemed right anymore; she couldn't just count the facts she knew were certain because Libby no longer knew what *certain* was.

Ultimately, it all came back to the train. It woke her again that night, shrill whistle slicing through the air, cutting a knife through the nightmare where she'd been stuck at the top of a Ferris wheel, listening to the two women argue far below while the structure creaked and rattled in the wind. This time, instead of attempting to return to sleep, she counted the whistles.

It was three, as it always was. A more superstitious person might have considered it some sort of omen, but Libby was too exhausted to think about superstitions. She settled for staring at her ceiling until the dawn rays of sun peeked through the curtains, greeting her with wispy warmth. Her head still pounded from her trip to Gerry's, but it wasn't anything some pain relievers couldn't fix — if she finally decided to take some.

Per Libby's request, Jacob left the morning before, after her failed attempt to take a walk. He had found her outside at the gate just staring down the street. He had to snap his fingers in front of her face to get her attention and bring her back in the house.

Once inside, the air between them was near-silent and tense. Libby didn't tell him that she had just had another nightmare out in the yard. The only sounds were small tinks coming from Jacob's spoon as he was finally able to start eating breakfast.

After he finished eating, Libby informed Jacob that he needed to leave. He protested a little, but Libby did not offer him an explanation. She did not feel that she owed him one, and she just wanted him gone. His sudden presence in Atheneum was a disturbance.

As he prepared to leave, Libby bid him only a quiet "Goodbye" as he opened her front door.

"Libby," he started, pausing at the threshold and turning to look at her. "I don't know what's going on with you or this town, but you'd tell me if something bigger was wrong, right?"

"Right," Libby thought, but even she didn't know anymore. Jacob took her silence as his answer and stepped out into the morning sun, pulling the door shut behind him. Moments later, Libby heard his car start and crunches in the gravel as he pulled away. She almost felt bad for sending him away so soon, but Libby couldn't shake the feeling that he'd been a special trigger for the nightmares yesterday. She had never had two nightmares in the same day, let alone two within about thirty minutes of each other. Now that she had another one during the night, she was convinced that she made the right decision to send him away. Libby was starting to see that she needed to trust her intuition a *bit* more than the people around her.

Ultimately, it came down to how much she wanted to distract herself. She had called Angela yesterday, and informed her that she would not be coming back to work just yet. Therefore, she didn't have work today as an option, so the next best thing would be to wander around the town. She figured she could now give pensive thought to the things that Jacob brought up yesterday.

With that decision in mind, Libby left her house and started for Thirp's, on the search for caffeine to start her day. She was out of coffee at home, and she knew she needed to go shopping, but that could wait until later.

The bell overhead chimed obnoxiously as Libby stepped into the store, but she'd grown used to it by now, and just greeted Thirp with as much cheerfulness as she could muster on a day like this. Libby headed straight to the coolers on the back wall of this section of the store, and started picking through the caffeinated ones. She was glad that Thirp had an assortment of beverages in his feed store.

"Oh," said a voice, familiar and snarky, just as she grabbed for an energy drink, "you're *still* here?"

Libby whirled around, coming face to face with Brandon Jade's scornful expression. Eyes narrowed and arms crossed, he glanced her up and down in a rather judging manner. Libby's first instinct was to angle herself away, as she was feeling exposed beneath his gaze. He had her cornered in, however, and there wasn't much room to get past him.

"I'm sorry," she replied, voice snipped, "I'm not sure what you mean. If you'd excuse me."

The fact was, Libby knew exactly what he meant. He was asking her why she was still in the town, still at HouBayou, and still in Texas in general. Libby didn't feel as though she really needed to satisfy his nosiness — not that it'd be possible to do that in the first place — so she made a move to step around him. Brandon slid back in front of her and hindered her efforts to get past him.

"Something tells me you know *exactly* what I'm talking about," he said, and paused before adding "Libby," in a firmer tone.
He changed to a Cajun drawl, all the while staring intently into her face. "All the way from the … Bayou. Yes … the old *Bayou*."

He went back to his regular dialect. "Listen, if you were just going to run all the way back home to mommy and daddy, why not just stay there? Make it easier for the rest of us, yeah?"

He smiled an easy smile that didn't quite touch his eyes. Libby knew in an instant that this was as insincere as it got in this town, and fury started to swell over her. She'd just come here for something to drink, and here she was being harassed by Brandon Jade. Again.

"Like it or not," Libby snapped. Her voice was somewhat loud, but she was not quite yelling. "Atheneum is my home now and I have every right to be here as the rest of you. Nothing you do or say is going to make me leave. *This* is where I want to be, and *this* is where I'm going to stay."

Brandon seemed none too pleased by Libby's sharp words, his expression hardening as if he wasn't used to people talking back to him. Especially her, being that she hadn't retorted earlier in the week when he had harsh words for her. Poppy had said the Jades were the most influential family in Atheneum, and she'd just talked back to one. Instantly, she was starting to regret that.

Just as Brandon opened his mouth, Fred Thirp stepped around the corner, mouth turned down. "Mr. Jade. Ms. Ferguson. Is there a problem here?"

"No," Brandon said, putting on an easy smile again. He turned around to face Fred. "There's no problem. I was just getting ready to leave when I ran into Ms. Ferguson here. We're not very well acquainted, so I thought I'd say hello."

Thirp seemed unsatisfied with the response, but he didn't say anything in challenge to Brandon. With the crow's feet at the edge of his eyes crinkling, he just grunted and turned away, and limped back towards the front out of Libby's sight. The moment he'd gone, Brandon turned on his heel so quickly that Libby jumped back.

"Watch who you talk to like that, little girl," Brandon bit out, "you're swimming in the deep end now."

Abandoning Libby against the drink coolers, Brandon whirled around and strode out without buying anything. The bell announced his leave, obnoxious chime again echoing in this small part of the store. The adrenaline in Libby's limbs drained, leaving her weak in the knees and far beyond regretful.

Thirp only side-eyed Libby when she made it to the front counter to make her purchase. "You be safe now," he grunted.

The reality of what she'd just done slammed into her once again. She could only manage a halfhearted nod in response and started out. All she could hope for now was that Brandon just had a lot of empty threats. Instead of dwelling on it and making herself more stressed, Libby opted to push the incident to the back of her mind for the time being and continued her walk down Holt Street.

Lorenzo G. Athens Park was a hop, skip, and a jump from Thirp's store. On most days, it seemed as though it went unused by the town's children, as Libby had noticed its emptiness on several occasions. She would have remained entirely oblivious to the park today had a familiar voice not called out to her as she walked by.

"Miss Libby!" Ruthie screeched, drawing Libby's attention to where the little girl hung upside down off the monkey bars. "Come play with me and Poppy!"

Sure enough, there was Poppy on the nearby bench, head lolling back, and eyes closed. Libby was just glad Ruthie seemed sensible enough not to run toward the street to get her attention. She thought, *"Where was her mother all the time?"* Nonetheless, Libby smiled and crossed the wood chips to join them.

"Hi, Ruthie," she greeted, "How are you?"

"Mommy had a meeting with a man so she said Poppy could take me to the park today!" Ruthie replied cheerfully, grinning from ear to ear.

As if his name had been a summon, Poppy woke with a start. "Ruthie? Ruthie May, where are—," he paused, attention focusing on Libby.

"Oh. Libby. When did you get here?"

"Just a moment ago," Libby told him, watching Ruthie scramble further down the monkey bars.

Poppy patted the bench beside him invitingly. "Right away, I can see you seem troubled," he commented when Libby sat down.

Ruthie abandoned the monkey bars in favor of the swings. Libby watched her go back and forth like a metronome on one of the olive-colored seats.

Troubled didn't even begin to cover it at this point — Libby was ridiculously far beyond that. Poppy was someone she could confide in, but it was more of a question of where to start than anything.

"Well," Libby began, and then everything came spilling out before she could even pause to think about it, "I've been having these awful nightmares, and my cousin came yesterday, but I can't shake the feeling he made them worse. I talked back to Brandon Jade at Thirp's just now, and I don't know *what* he's planning to do, but—"

Poppy laughed. It startled Libby so much that she stopped mid-sentence, raising her eyes to stare back at the elderly man. It was a wholehearted laugh, made of shaking shoulders and wheezing breaths. Libby wasn't sure why he was laughing, but all she could really do was stare incredulously at him until he calmed down.

"Of course you'd be the one to talk back to Jade." He chuckled. "He probably deserved it. Didn't know what to do with himself, I'd reckon. Spoiled boys like him aren't used to people snapping back at them. I wouldn't worry too much, Libby."

Libby opened her mouth to protest, but Poppy carried on.

"I wouldn't think he'd mention that to anyone. Brandon Jade is known for causin' trouble, but admitting he'd let you get away with talking back would be like admitting defeat. That boy's a coward. He won't go complaining to Wilson or anything, that's for sure. You just keep chugging along and don't give him the time of day. Brandon Jade just wants his ego fed like a child."

Poppy's words felt as if they'd instantly lifted a burden from Libby's shoulders. She breathed a sigh of relief, although her shoulders still slumped. Her panic about Brandon seemed pointless already — she was glad she'd encountered Poppy so early in the day, otherwise it would have been awful going around all day with the thoughts on her mind.

"Thank you, Poppy," Libby said.

"Nothing to thank me for," Poppy waved a hand dismissively. "Now, what's this about nightmares?"

Libby dove into an explanation about the recurring nightmares, withholding few details. Poppy's gaze followed Ruthie while Libby talked, but she could tell by the expressions on his features that he was still listening to her. Once Libby had finished talking, Poppy sat in contemplative silence a moment longer.

"It seems like you've got some unconfronted trauma in your past," he finally said, "and something about Atheneum is forcing you to try facing it after all this time."

"But why now of all times?" Libby knew, rationally, that something had been drawing her to this town since she arrived. It felt like she was meant to be in Atheneum, despite the way the locals treated her. As hard as it was to get past the poor treatment, Libby couldn't shake the feeling that there was something bigger than herself going on here.

"Who knows?" Poppy sat back. "Fate, coincidence, your job. It could be anything." Libby was struck with the memory of their conversation about the town's history — the Jades and the Sleuths. She hadn't gotten to tell him at the time; she wasn't supposed to know about it, but her family name was Sleuth.

"Poppy," she started again, "I don't think I'm supposed to know this, but my name ... my family's name. It's-"

A car came screeching up to the curb. Ruthie immediately dug her feet into the wood chips, eyes brightening. Poppy's expression, on the other hand, became sullen and dark. It clicked to Libby just as Ruthie shouted it.

"Mommy!" Ruthie screamed, racing towards the car.

The woman who stepped out was someone who Libby had seen before, but only from a distance. She leaned down to pat Ruthie's head and gestured her quickly into the car, before marching across the space between herself and Libby and Poppy. Her eyes, dark and intense, locked onto Libby.

Libby was admittedly intimidated by the severe looking woman, dressed down in a dark suit, with equally dark hair tied back in a prim bun. She looked as if she hadn't smiled in years, and certainly wasn't beaming when she approached Libby.

"Bonnie," Poppy started, getting up. "Hang on."

"Get in the car, Dad," the woman snapped, "and take that ridiculous tie off!" Libby had been so preoccupied by her encounter with Brandon, that she had not noticed that Poppy was once again wearing the same damaged green tie that his daughter had cut at the Barbecue Ball.

Poppy looked taken aback by the woman's sharp tone towards him. Maybe he reacted that way just because they were in public, because Libby felt certain that this woman probably always treated her father in this manner at home.

Libby flinched when Bonnie's gaze immediately moved back to her. Bonnie jabbed a finger in Libby's face, with her eyebrows lowered, and lips drawn in a half snarl.

"And *you* stay away!" she yelled at Libby. "You stay away from my *father*, and you stay away from my *daughter*! If I ever, *ever* catch you near one of them again, I will make your life *miserable!*"

Without even waiting for Libby's response, Bonnie whipped around and stomped back to the car. Poppy glanced apologetically at Libby.

"Sorry about her," he murmured, "Bonnie isn't normally like this. She—"

"*Dad!*" Bonnie shouted from outside of the car.

"I'd best be going," Poppy said. He quickly added in a lowered voice, "you know where to find me."

"But she said—" Libby began.

Poppy shook his head. "I decide who I see and who I don't," he informed Libby, before hurrying after Bonnie and Ruthie.

Libby watched him go, at a loss. She didn't want to be on Bonnie's bad side any more than she already was, and to make matters worse, she didn't know *why* she was on Bonnie's bad side to begin with. Libby was baffled, but everyone else in this town seemed to know everything about everybody. Brandon somehow knew that she had gone to see her parents. Old Man Ferguson obviously knew her full name. And now Bonnie had some reason for wanting Libby to keep her distance.

For a second, Poppy had made it seem like the day was going to turn out fine, but Libby was seriously doubting that now.

Once the car had hauled out of sight, Libby sighed and resigned herself to going shopping. She'd have to do it eventually, and she supposed there was no time like the present to get it done. She was keeping with her goal of having something to keep her busy and distracted.

Shopping, as it turned out, was the most uneventful part of the day, because her mind kept going back to Brandon and Poppy, Ruthie, and Bonnie. All day she wondered, *"Is it really a good idea to still go see Poppy?"*

By the time she got home that night, exhaustion had already claimed her body, turning her limbs to lead. Her eyes drooped as she put everything up and stumbled into her bedroom, only barely managing to convince herself to change into some night clothes before she collapsed in bed.

She just hoped she wouldn't have any nightmares, and her wish was granted. She woke again early the next morning, still feeling exhausted, but at least she hadn't had any nightmares.

Then — with a start — Libby sat straight up, realization and horror washing over her.

She'd slept through the whole night.

The late-night train hadn't come.

Chapter Nine
by Mickie Ezzo

The day started off easy at first. Libby decided to dismiss the midnight train for the time being, although she couldn't stop herself from wondering about it every now and again. She wanted to satiate her appetite for the morning, so she headed out of the house to Thirp's for coffee, with plans to follow that with a short stroll.

With this break that she had from her dreaded position at HouBayou, she again pondered the thought of quitting and moving onto another job. How that would come off to her superiors, she didn't care. But the idea of having to put up with a different position and different mean people didn't sound entirely appealing to her either. Given she did have a good amount of money saved from working at the company, she wondered if she could just take a break entirely from working and enjoy herself.

Would it be worth it? She contemplated this a little longer as she gave Fred Thirp a half-hearted wave goodbye as she strode out the door and into the breezy, sunny morning.

The breeze did feel good to her as it was pretty hot already for nine in the morning. The sidewalks were a bit cracked with weeds and plants poking through, but Libby had the path memorized so much so that she knew where to step up, and where to watch her step down without even looking. For the first time, she wanted to relish the day and see the clear, blue sky. Gosh, it was gorgeous. A few clouds were scattered far apart, but not enough to wonder if it would rain. Maybe since she was still mostly in a melancholy mood, she did however, feel that some rain was definitely needed.

Seeing the park nearby, she decided to get on the swing set. It had been quite some time since she had done that, so she headed over, and plopped down in a blue one that was a couple swings away from some children who were having a good time giggling and swinging on their stomachs. One young boy held his arms out while he swung back and forth, looking like Superman.

This amused her a bit and she hid her smile, wondering if she'd bump into Poppy and Ruthie here. In that moment, she recollected the situation from the day before. Now her stomach turned at the thought of sticking around. Yet something seemed to call to her to see Poppy.

Why though? She didn't want to see Ruthie's mother again. Tied between a rock and a hard place, she found herself pushing her feet gently off the ground to give a little swing. As she swung, her thoughts of seeing Poppy swung back and forth as well. Finally, she pushed off and stood up, then found her feet taking her in the direction of the library.

It took her a good few minutes to make her way into town and spot the library from a distance. Her heart pounded in her chest as she grew fearful of her choice to confront Poppy with the threat of his daughter, Bonnie. Yet her gut was pulling her ever closer to the doors of the library. She followed her feet inside the building and welcomed the temporary peace and tranquility of the building. Just seeing the books somehow gave her a comfort and solace of the quiet. Somehow, she felt that no Jade or any other person in power could really get a hold of her here.

Feeling a little more courageous in her presence at the library, she made her way to the elevator and rode it up to the second floor where she had last met with Poppy. In her thoughts, she prayed he would be there so she could ask a few questions she had running around in her mind.

As she strode past the shelves of books, she ran her hand along the bindings of the books on her left-hand side, feeling the sentimentality of the moment. There were whispers going about the building which made her relish the library-esque feeling even more. But those sounds were distant, and she did not see any other people on this floor. As she grew closer to the target area, she heard whispers escalating a bit to normal voices. And one was a dreadful tone she knew. This made her gut drop.

Instinctively, she dropped down behind a fully stacked shelf, just barely peeping through the cracks between the shelf and the books underneath it to just get a glimpse of the loathsome — *Brandon Jade*. He was unhappily accompanied by Poppy.

The look of animosity on Brandon's face made Libby tremble in fear as he raised his voice, shaking a book she'd seen before. He said, "This book doesn't deserve to be on these shelves and you know it, sir. You of all people should've known better than to write and publish it. I couldn't exactly stop you from writing it. But just letting people like … Libby … read this stuff is ludicrous."

The icy, bitter tone of his voice when he spoke her name made her shiver before he continued. "She has no part or share in any of this town. Atheneum will *never* be her home. Don't encourage a foreigner to read this stuff. I have a right to burn this book as I find necessary."

The anger in his voice made Libby furious that he would take that tone to an elderly man. Then she thought, *How in the world did he know I had read the book? Or much less know the story? I never said anything about any of it — except to Poppy.*

Then Poppy spoke up to Brandon in a chiding tone, "Now you listen to me, young man. You have no place to disrespect who I talk to and who I don't talk to. If I feel that the story needs to be out and about, then it should stay in the library. I don't even know how you knew she read it, or I even told her the story."

"Well maybe you need to pay attention to what you say to your granddaughter," Brandon said slyly, a smile coming through his voice. "And don't forget that I also saw you talking to Libby outside of the Barbecue Ball."

A sly snake at that, Libby thought, sneering at this whole thing. Yet her concern for Poppy was still high. Could he really get out of this without getting banned from the town? Or worse?

Her brows furrowed, but she still chose to remain hidden where she was just three shelves away from their distance. Poppy defended himself yet again, "I don't ever tell Ruthie anything that would put her in harm's way."

"Then why did Bonnie literally beat her just to get that information for me? Huh?" Brandon jeered. "Ruthie was more than happy to tell her mother after a few licks and many harsh words."

Libby could see the deep red flush on Poppy's face and she swore that he had growled as he spoke low, "You really did that much damage to a poor little girl just to see what you can hold against one outsider? You don't even know Libby Ferguson at all. Shame on you, young man. You have enough strings in this town to make anyone dance, but you sure will never have me on a string. If I have to, I'll take whatever I need to avoid this town. Besides Ruthie, there's nothing for me here, and you can't hold that hostage against me."

"Oh, so you'll run?" Libby could hear a bit of the creepy excitement coming from Brandon's voice.

"I don't know what game you want to play, and I know it seems like I just said that, but I will not run away," Poppy retorted. "Not like Miriam did when your lot chased her off. She had every right to escape. But I know everything about this case and can prevent you from taking anything you greedy Jades want. I have the information that no other person does."

Poppy was very sure of himself and Libby wondered why he had never cared to share that tidbit of information. What else did Poppy know?

Right then, she realized that he'd showed all of his cards.

She knew as Brandon laughed cruelly, whispering, "Well, you've played right into my hands, you old geezer." He made a gesture and it felt like all the sounds in the building stopped. Libby felt the tension thicken as men suddenly came from certain corners and started venturing towards Poppy. Libby was horrified as she watched three men grab Poppy's arms and tie his wrists with rope. Panicked, she knew that he was being taken hostage. But it was getting too close now. She was way too near, and she started backing away, remaining hidden as best as she could. Brandon then called out, "That goes for you as well, Libby. It's about time I got to play these games again. And, oh, how I've missed them."

As Libby backed up slowly, she saw Brandon's steely, sickening gaze slowly meet hers through the stacks, and she realized she'd played right into his hands. He laughed as she suddenly felt hands grab her arms. Instantly, she started screaming, but it only lasted until she felt a sack being pulled over her head. She could see nothing and only felt hands binding her up with rope and covering her nose and mouth with a damp rag that smelled strongly of chloroform. She knew that smell from bottles that her parents had at their practice in Lacassine.

Soon, she was out.

***

"Wake up!" a harsh voice shouted, following through with a strong pinch to her cheek. "Wake up, you ..."

Brandon Jade. All she could remember was him and his strong, steely gaze. Her cheek swelled with pain and her head rolled to the side. Her eyelids felt heavy and she lolled her head to the other side, trying to lift it up. Once more, she felt a pinch on her cheek and she winced in pain.

"Wake up!"

"Libby," Poppy's voice cut through to her and she jolted awake then. He sounded as though he was in pain and her concern skyrocketed. Perking up really fast, she felt herself jolt against the ties of the ropes on her wrists and noted that she was sitting in a metal chair. Her skirt was splayed about her legs and her shirt collar was mussed. Her were legs strapped to the legs of the chair and her wrists were bound behind her back, tape over her mouth.

Her eyesight slowly gained focus, as well as her brain, which still felt groggy from the strong, odorous chemical. She found herself in a dark room that was about ten by twelve foot with an interrogation lamp shining over a metal table. This made her think that they were at the police station, but chances of that were slim. Then again, everyone was in the Jades' pockets.

Angela's voice resounded in her head, *"If you can't beat 'em, join 'em."*

Heaving a sigh, she glanced sorrowfully at Poppy whose face was swollen and puffy. *They'd hit him? They beat him*! Horror-struck, she gasped underneath the tape, and felt pain in her solar plexus. She longed to wrap her arm around her chest to suppress the pain. Tears filled her eyes as she muffled an, "I'm sorry, Poppy."

"No," Poppy said, somehow knowing exactly what she said. "It's my fault. I shouldn't have written the book at all. I should've known that would be my undoing."

"Ain't that the truth," Brandon used his Cajun drawl then stood straight, wearing a black t-shirt that clung to his body, arms crossed over his chest, sneering at the two of them. "Now, since I have one impending death and another one possibly lining up, I think I'm having fun. I would like to interrogate both of you first. See that you don't be stupid." His gaze had shifted right to her and she knew that last statement was intended for her.

"And what if we don't comply?" Poppy gruffly responded, coughing.

"If?" Brandon scoffed at this. "Oh, if you don't comply, I'll torture you until you do."

Libby saw a light in Poppy's eyes which surprised her a bit as he spoke, "Young man, I'll have you know I've fought in World War II and served my time in 'Nam. I'm a soldier and a doctor, so I know all the torture methods and have trained other men who had minds as crazy as yours ... Don't you think for a second you can torment anything out of me."

Brandon narrowed his eyes, but still remained his snobby self. "Don't you try and dominate this situation, *old* man. This is my interrogation and I will not give into your ways. Besides, I already know you served, and I'll have you know I can change my intentions of torturing *you* physically," he said while pointing at Poppy. Slowly his gaze shifted back to Libby, and Poppy's eyes welled with tears, realizing the depth of the situation.

Libby then shook with fear. *They intended torture on her*! For what? She whimpered, but couldn't speak. Brandon seemed to only just suddenly note the tape, and proceeded to rip it right off her mouth. It left a tingling, burning sensation, and she whimpered again. Parting her lips, she managed to gasp for more breath. Brandon swaggered his head from one victim to the other, a smile playing on his curled lips. "I will get what I want from both of you or else you'll suffer the consequences."

Libby dared to find her voice yet stuttered, "What-what c-could I poss-possibly have to-to tell yo-you? I know-know nothing."

Brandon's eyes fixed on her and made his way to her until he hovered over her small frame. His hands slowly traced along her jawline and she turned away from the feeling of his fingertips on her skin. "Oh, I know you know nothing, woman. It's him who does — but you're the only way to get it out of him."

"Libby—" Poppy started to say, but she cut him off, making up her mind.

She said, "No, Poppy, let him. I can take it. I will take it if I have to."

"Libby," he spoke more softly to her now. "I know what this man will do to you and it's not worth the information I have for him."

She refused to hear it. "No, I'll take it. I have been through worse. I can do this."

"No," Poppy wouldn't hear it. "You don't have to." Then he directed his attention to Brandon. "I'll tell you what you want. Just let her go."

Brandon seemed to giggle with delight at all this. "Oh, it's so precious when they do this. Try to fend for the other. I've been through this before. I've watched my father torture the others, but I'll get to do it this time. Let's not forget who else should be in play."

The door next to the double paned mirror opened, revealing Wilson whose face looked bright and cheery, rubbing his hands together. "Okay, so who goes first?" he asked.

"You're late brother," Brandon sniffed at him without facing him.

"Well, sorry, but I had to make excuses for your current disappearance, which wasn't as easy this time. Apparently, that Angela woman is a piece of work. She should have never been put in that position," Wilson snapped, running his hands through his hair. His sinister gaze shifted to Libby and he seemed to have an idea, raising one brow at her. "Hey, I think you told me you owe me a new suit after that cup of coffee."

Libby blinked a couple of times before Brandon grabbed her chin, biting out, "Don't you remember spilling coffee on him all that time ago?"

As her mind spun, she realized what they were talking about and couldn't believe the audacity of it all. Brandon let go of her chin and she said, "Are you two serious right now?"

That was her mistake.

Wilson strode right over to her and stepped hard on her left foot. She moaned from the smarting pain that ensued there. Despite the ache, she managed to situate herself again more comfortably.

She dared to ask, "Pinching. Stepping on feet. Kind of childish, don't ya think?"

Wilson then grinned and grabbed his chance. He lightly stroked her face a bit, where it was reddened from Brandon's earlier pinches. "Oh, honey, we can do so much more than that."

"Leave her alone!" Poppy barked out. "I already told you I would cough up the information for you."

Wilson's eyes widened with delight. "Ooh, the old man wasn't too hard to crack then, huh, brother?"

Brandon snipped at Wilson. "Leave it to me, Will. I got this."

"Wait, wait, wait, you didn't tell me. How did this happen again?" Wilson was way too eager for something, and that bided Libby some time as she struggled with her restraints. She wished that she hadn't put on a skirt that didn't have pockets. She could've managed to wear something more suitable to store her Swiss army knife. Too bad. It was all the way back at her house sitting on the bedside table. She hoped that Greystroke wouldn't cut himself on it. She thought, *Boy, that was a random thought to have of my cat.*

Brandon interrupted her thoughts, saying, "So we have two hostages because I was chiding the old man for his stupidity in writing that dastardly book, and Libby just happened to be witness to it. She thought I didn't know."

This made Wilson laugh like a schoolgirl. Cracking his knuckles, he said, "So you've gotten them broken in for now and we just need to extract the information. Start talking, Poppy." He mocked him in the last sentence.

Brandon snapped at his brother, grabbing him by both shoulders and shaking him. He bit out, "It's my job to interrogate — not you."

He followed through by going over to Poppy, and Libby watched as he tipped the chair back, Poppy's hair falling backwards a bit. "So, where is the last heir? Huh? I know you know. Spit it out, geezer. I need that land."

Suddenly, it all clicked and Libby realized that Poppy knew.

Wait? Poppy knew? How though? She grew flustered as Wilson recovered and managed to say, "So you know his location?"

"Yes," Poppy croaked.

Now Libby struggled and wanted so desperately to get out of there; but at the same time, her mind whirled at how in the world Poppy knew. *Just how? And why did he say it was a he?*

Brandon shoved his head in the direction of her. "Will, you handle her? I've got this man to talking now."

Her lips trembled in fear as she watched Will eye her in a weird way, and she cringed at the vibes she was getting. *No way would he ever*!

But he did. He brushed his hands along her arm and slowly reached for her face. Refusing to look into his eyes, she felt his fingers slowly trace up her arm and reach for her neck, slowly pressing against her trachea. She felt like he was trying to let her know that he could hurt her much more than he or Brandon already had.

He got in her face, licked her right cheek, but then backed off. Looking disgusted, with his tongue still hanging out, he said, "Why does she taste like chemical?"

It didn't take long before his eyes rolled in the back of his head, and he passed out. Relieved of this, Libby shifted her terrified gaze to Brandon, who glanced back at his brother's crumpled form on the ground and rolled his eyes. He muttered something that Libby couldn't understand, but she knew they weren't pleasant words.

He then returned his gaze to Poppy. Libby couldn't see his face, as Brandon was blocking her vision. However, she could tell that he still had the chair tilted back, towering in front of Poppy's face.

"So who is he? Where has he run away? Tell me!" Brandon yelled.

The labored breaths of Poppy came through as he spoke, "Louisiana. He's in ... Louisiana."

"Where in Louisiana? That's just the state, man."

Praying hard that he wouldn't say what she was thinking, she closed her eyes tightly, wanting all of this gone. Poppy's voice spoke hoarsely,

"New Orleans. He doesn't live there; but he's visiting there right now."

"What's his name?" Brandon demanded, making Poppy's chair screech a little bit on the cement flooring.

"Samson Sleuth. His name is Samson Sleuth. He's in New Orleans for some kind of conference. I don't know how long though," Poppy moaned out.

Suddenly, she grew completely confused that she almost dared to wonder aloud, but clamped her mouth shut. *What was Poppy doing*? Opening her eyes, she stared at the ceiling, hearing Brandon drop the chair back on all four feet, thudding loudly. She glanced at Wilson's form which still lay limp. Brandon turned around, facing her now, looking grim. "Too bad he told me already — I was looking forward to torturing you. I guess that means I have to get rid of both of you now. Neither of you are of help anymore."

Poppy chuckled at this and Brandon swung back over to him, biting out, "What's so funny, old man?"

"That's the biggest mistake you could ever make," Poppy croaked out. "You need us more than you know." Libby saw the sparkle in his eyes, and she saw Brandon's eyes darken at Poppy's words.

Confusion must have filtered into his mind and he dared to ask, "Why would I need either one of you?"

"My daughter knows full well that if I up and die now, she'll know it was you," he said. "And given she's one of you, that means a civil war between y'all. And if Libby dies, that's gonna definitely bring up suspicion, as she's just an outsider. You Jades have only been known to do away with those who 'helped' you build your town. If Libby is taken out in this way, Angela will raise a stink along with everyone else. I know you're not that much of a moron, Brandon Jade." Poppy laughed at all of this.

This surprised Libby and she glanced at Brandon who frowned at his words. "Then I'll just have to keep both of you hostage, or else you'll both squawk on me." He glanced at her, and she felt concern once more as he slowly let a grin play on his face. "I like playing, but I do have manners. As they say, 'ladies first'."

He stepped towards her, his fingers rubbing the gold band of his emerald ring. Her eyes widened in horror as she saw him lift his right arm up over her head.

Chapter Ten
by Ann James

Libby moaned. Images of Aunt Melanie and her mother standing toe to toe, their faces contorted in rage, their voices loud played through her mind like an old black and white movie. It felt so real, how could it not be? Once again, she was a child on a boat deck, the continual rolling from side to side causing her stomach to churn. She tossed her head, then gasped. A stab of pain ripping her cheek dragged her out of that nightmare into another — this physical one that might prove to be far worse.

Her initial instinct was to reach for her cheek and do something to ease the pain, but it wasn't only her restraints that stopped her. She widened her eyes, as there was nothing but darkness around her, and she didn't know if she was alone. She took slow, deep breaths, trying to focus, and put those last upsetting images out of her mind.

Where am I?

She struggled to understand what was going on, as well as gain some recognition of her whereabouts. But all she could remember was walking to the library. After that — nothing.

She was tied to a chair, so she knew she was in some kind of danger. There was a steady ache in her arms, as she tried to shift her position. The rope chafed at her skin with every movement. It was the same in her legs, with soreness resonating from her waist down to her feet.

Libby was scared — so scared that she was sure someone would hear her heart as it thundered in her chest. She turned her head back to the left and saw a strip of faint light coming from under what she assumed was the door. A door leading to where, she wondered. The air smelled old and moldy, closed in, like there were no windows. She took a breath and smelled something else, something coppery. Blood, she thought. Even without being able to touch it, she was aware of a stickiness on her cheek.

From somewhere outside of the room she picked up the hum of people talking. The voices were deep, probably male. Somehow, they seemed familiar, but at this second, she couldn't place them. Whoever they were, it probably wasn't good news for her. She tried to make out their words and failed. After a couple of minutes, the conversation ended. For what seemed like forever, Libby waited, not daring to move. Were they gone? Please let them be gone, she prayed.

The door creaked and then opened. Libby's heart skipped a beat, and she quickly dropped her chin to her chest. Even though her back was to the door, she closed her eyes and pretended she was still unconscious.

"The old man and that foolish girl are still out of it."

It was Brandon Jade's voice. He and his brother, Wilson Jade entered the small room, leaving the door open behind them. For a few seconds they said nothing. Libby's pulse raced.

"And from the looks of them, we'll have plenty of time to get home and have dinner before they wake up. I'm starved," Brandon continued.

"Hungry!" Wilson said. "You must be kidding. Between you shaking the dillweed out of me, and then me passing out from the chloroform, food is the last thing on my mind. My head feels like it's going to explode. I swear, if you ever shake me like that again, bro ... I'll ..."

"You'll what?" Brandon asked. His tone was harsh, and Libby could well imagine the look on his face. She'd seen his ugly sneer on more than one occasion.

"You won't do anything," Brandon continued to taunt. "Who's kidding who?"

"Look, bro, I don't want to fight. And the way I feel right now, I wouldn't stand a chance against you," Wilson said.

"You got that right," Brandon replied. "And you still couldn't beat me even on your best day." He laughed, but it wasn't a happy sound.

Since it seemed as though the brothers were occupied with their own conversation and not focused on her, Libby mustered enough courage to crack her left eye open, just the tiniest bit.

From the corner of her eye, she could see that Brandon was about two yards away from her on that side, and Wilson stood by the door, just barely inside the room. There was a lantern on the floor. Lilly could see Wilson clench his fists, but he kept his arms by his side. Even in her restricted vision, she could see the look he gave his brother was one of pure venom.

No love lost there, she thought. Libby almost felt sorry for him. It couldn't have been easy for Wilson growing up with Brandon for a younger brother. Still, she would have felt a great deal more sympathetic to Wilson if he hadn't played a part in this shoddy, little scheme. Bits and pieces had already started coming back to her.

"Let's get going," Brandon said.

"Fine," Wilson replied. He turned to walk out, but the slight movement must have cause him some discomfort because he immediately stopped and groaned, rubbing his forehead. "Darn that hurts."

Surprisingly, this appeared to garner a little sympathy from his sibling.

"Hey, ease up why don't you," Brandon said. He flashed his brother his legendary grin, the one which always seemed to get him what he wanted, and patted Wilson's shoulder. "You know I didn't mean to hurt you, it was just for show. To get that stupid old man to tell us where the latest Sleuth heir is hanging out."

Wilson snorted. "Sure, sure. And how did that work out?"

"You better watch your mouth," Brandon snarled.

"You're right, Brandon. I'm sure he'll talk some more. Give us more info about this Samson character. Sooner, rather than later."

"Well let's get going. Or did that headache make you already forget dinner?"

Wilson shuddered. "Dinner?" He shook his head. "Sorry, bro, I already told you I'm not interested."

"Stop whining," Brandon said. He reached into his back pocket and pulled out a small flashlight and then flicked it on "Hurry it up."

"I'm doing my best."

"Don't be such a wuss!" Brandon ordered.

"How'd you get here? To the library I mean," Wilson asked his brother as they stepped into the dark hall outside of the room.

"Walked. I didn't want to advertise my presence."

"Since I was running late, I drove. My car is parked in the library lot," Wilson said. "It will look very odd if someone sees it parked there after regular business hours. Especially on a Saturday."

"Good thinking. For once," Brandon smirked. "Yeah. Let's drive that away from here. But I promise, you won't want to miss dinner. One of my old buddies is here."

"Who," Wilson asked, wondering why Brandon would invite someone over while all this was going on.

"JJ," Brandon replied.

He shut the door behind them. The sound of their voices faded.

Don't lock it, Libby thought, but she heard the click of the lock and sighed. What now, she wondered. She listened, hoping the brothers would enjoy a very lengthy dinner, giving her time to figure out exactly how she was going to get out of this room. It was eerily quiet, but after several seconds she became aware of the steady drone of someone, not her, breathing.
Poppy?

In a rush, it all came back. She'd gone to the library hoping to meet him, to learn more of the town's secrets. Instead she found Brandon Jade threatening him and somehow, both she and Poppy had ended up here, held captive in a small dark room. Somewhere? But where?

For sure, this was not the same room they were in before. This room was at least double the size.

She craned her head toward the sound of the breathing. He was in a chair a few feet behind her, facing the opposite way.

"Poppy," she whispered. "Are you awake? Can you hear me?"

There was no response. She remembered that he had bruising on his face and this infuriated her. How dare Brandon, a big, strong man in his prime do this to Poppy? *Coward*, she thought.

Another memory surfaced. The one of Wilson, the older and not so handsome, not so accomplished brother touching her face. She gagged. They had to get out of here before the pair of lunatic brothers returned.

Libby attempted to move her hands, but the rope was so tight she was only able to move them a few inches. Her thumb brushed against a protrusion, something hard and ridged, sharp at the end. A screw, she thought. Perfect!

Readjusting her position, she began rubbing the rope against the screw, doing her best to avoid contact with her wrist. "Ouch!" The screw nicked her skin. She moved slower and more carefully causing the activity to take longer than she would have liked. She grew more and more anxious with each passing second. Eventually, and with a minimum of blood, the rope split, freeing her hands.

She looked back at Poppy before reaching down to her ankles. She tugged at the rope, worrying the knot. Finally, it gave way.

Libby rushed over to Poppy. His chin rested on his chest. His eyes were closed. A trickle of blood stained his cheek, and she gently rubbed next to it. "Wake up," she said. "Please wake up."

He groaned.

"Thank goodness," she said, continuing to stroke his face. "It's me, Poppy. It's Libby."
His eyes opened, but barely. "What happened?" he asked.

While she undid his hands and ankles she explained what she remembered, hoping it was everything.

"Please tell me you have some idea of where we are," she said when she managed to free him.

He rubbed his wrists and glanced around the room. "I believe I do know. The founding families built a series of tunnels under Atheneum. I think we're in one of them."

Libby was dumbfounded. "Have you been here before?"

Poppy shrugged. "Yes. This looks like the same room I was in. It was back when I was doing research for my book."

"Why in the world would they do that? Why would someone want tunnels?" Libby asked.

"During the first part of the twentieth century, all four of the families had a hand in secretly building these under the town," Poppy said. "If I remember correctly, this room was built as a storage area for the Threadgood family. You probably didn't realize that the library was constructed on the former site of their home. And the passageway ..." Poppy pointed to the door, "tunnel is still probably the best word — well from here it runs south, connecting it to the main Jade estate. The one where they hold the Barbecue Ball. The tunnel's north leg goes under Atheneum's town hall. Slightly further on, it connects to the bank and further still, the railroad office. Beyond that point, the tunnels are impassable."

"Why?" Libby asked, trying to make some kind of sense of what Poppy was saying. *Atheneum is certainly a strange place*, she thought.

"A flood during the sixties caused the walls of the tunnel to collapse and they have never been rebuilt," Poppy explained. "It was believed the portion of the tunnel that collapsed connected to the Sleuth estate, but no one in town knows for sure."

"Or no one who is willing to say," Libby concluded. Her thoughts went back to Brandon and Wilson. No doubt they were familiar with them.

"The original purpose of the tunnels," Poppy continued, "was to provide easy access for the founding families to get together, enabling them to concoct their schemes and execute their plans for the town in secret. I believe the Jade family are currently the only ones in Atheneum who use them. I've heard they find the passageways an ideal location to hide cash and other valuables. They are also useful in the performance of other nefarious activities, like kidnapping and such."

"We can attest to that," Libby said.

"Secret meetings, shady business, and ..." His hands began to shake. "Think of all those dead Sleuths."

Libby took hold of his hands to steady them, looking into his pale blue eyes. "You know, don't you?" she asked. "My mother's maiden name is Sleuth."

"I suspected." Poppy nodded. The look on his face was grim.

"Why?"

"There's a photo of one of your ancestors in my book. You look exactly like her. When we get out of here, I'll show you." Poppy looked around the room. His shoulders slumped. "If we get out."

"We'll get out," Libby said, sounding more positive than she felt. She reached into her pocket, hoping against hope Brandon had not checked for her phone, but no such luck.

"Don't move, Poppy," she said. "We have that lantern there, but it's not letting us see much. I'm going to see if there is a light switch in here like the other room."

"Careful," he said. "And just a word of warning. You should be even more cautious when we get out of here. Sleuths don't do well around here, don't forget that."

"You know more about that than you've already said, don't you?"

"Yes, but not now. I'd rather go with your optimism of us finding a way out of this room before they come back."

Libby nodded and got up, walking the perimeter of the room, feeling the walls as she went. She found nothing except for dust and a few cobwebs — something which did not bear thinking about since she had an aversion to spiders.

Sighing, she peered through the gloom and decided to check out the door. The knob didn't seem to be anything fancy so maybe she'd get lucky. She felt her pockets, wishing her small card wallet would miraculously reveal itself.

"Hey, Poppy. You wouldn't happen to have a credit card or something like that, would you?" she asked, not expecting a positive response.

Poppy chuckled. "Are you some kind of super-thief or something?"

"Not exactly. But when I was a kid, I saw someone on TV open a locked door using a credit card," she responded. "One day when I accidentally locked myself out of the house, I tried it and darn if it didn't work."

"I'm not surprised. You have a ton of spunk." Poppy reached into his back pocket. "No," he said, shaking his head. "Brandon must have helped himself. Sorry."

Libby sighed. "That's okay."

"But wait," Poppy said, suddenly sounding excited. "This might work." He extracted a card from his shirt pocket and waved it. "My library card."

"Perfect!" Libby reached for the plastic card. "Fingers crossed."

"Piece of cake," Poppy replied and they both laughed.

Libby inserted the card into the narrow space between the strike plate and the jamb. She slid it up and down several times before she heard a soft click. "I think I've got it." After mentally crossing all of her fingers, she reached for the knob and was able to turn it.

"Voila!" She pulled open the door and waved her hand. "We're out of here, Poppy!"

Poppy struggled to his feet, holding the back of the metal chair for balance.

"Wait, let me help you." She reached for him, placing one of his arms around her shoulder, after she'd grabbed and held the lantern with her other hand. "We've got this."

Together, they stepped into the passageway. Libby crinkled her nose. "Yuck. It smells so moldy. It would probably be better to get out of here as quickly as possible. Do you have any idea exactly where we are, Poppy?"

"As I said, I believe we're under the library, but that's a guess."

"I've got an idea. Why don't you wait here for a bit while I see if I can find stairs or a door to the outside world?"

"Good thinking."

He seems tired, Libby thought. She set off, walking steadily for about five minutes before deciding to try the opposite direction. Running, she arrived back where she'd left Poppy in no time. He was propped up against the wall.

"You okay?" She tried to catch her breath.

"I'm fine. Any luck?"

Libby shook her head. "But don't worry. We'll be long gone before the brothers Jade make their reappearance."

Poppy nodded. "Once we get our bearings, it shouldn't be far. If I'm right and we're under the library, that is."

Libby squeezed Poppy's hand. "I'll be right back." She made her way along the dark passageway as quickly as she could. She was worried about so many things. First, Poppy didn't look well. He needed to rest and that couldn't happen until they were out of there. Secondly, if Poppy was right and this tunnel was located under the library, undoubtedly Brandon and Wilson would make their reappearance somewhere in this area. She and Poppy had to be gone before this happened.

Libby's guardian angel must have been looking out for her because as soon as she turned the corner, she spotted a staircase. She ran up, taking the stairs two at a time. At the top, she discovered a storage room, filled with cases of old, dusty books. There was a door in the corner, blocked by several cartons. She moved the boxes aside and was elated to find the door actually opened. Directly beyond the room was a small hallway leading to an outside door. After exiting that one, she paused for an instant, taking in the sight of the twinkling stars.

"Thank you, thank you," she murmured as she turned and rushed back to Poppy.

"I found it, a staircase just around the corner. It leads to a door that will take us outside," she told him.

"Good girl," Poppy said. He leaned on her and the two made their way up the stairs and outside as quickly as they were able. When the library door slammed behind them, they paused and sucked in the night air.

"This is heaven," Libby said.

"Agreed." Poppy leaned heavily on his companion. It was clear he'd about reached his physical limit.

"Just a little farther," Libby said. "Once we're out of this parking lot, there is a short walk, not more than a block, and then we'll be shielded by the trees. From there, the trail follows the railroad tracks."

Poppy nodded. Of course he already knew this.

Libby turned off the lantern. She helped Poppy across the pavement and into the street. They had almost reached the path leading into the trees when, in the distance, Libby heard a car motor.

Her heart rate sped up. "Someone is coming. Hurry."

Libby guided Poppy up the path, pushing aside stray branches and moss to help clear his way. They had just stepped into the shelter of the foliage when the car zoomed past them, careening into the library parking lot, its occupants illuminated by a street light.

It was a silver BMW. Brandon Jade was at the wheel, and Wilson was in the backseat.

Sitting beside Brandon was someone else.

Chapter Eleven
by C. S. Sandlin

Shadows seemed to swallow their faces as Poppy and Libby kept going toward the railroad track. Libby slid slightly when they reached the dip just prior to the tracks. She slammed her knee against a thin trunk as she caught herself.

Poppy sighed. "Knew they were going to bring that soft soap cousin of yours into this. Everyone's on a leash in this town."

Libby's patience cracked. "More like at sword's point. And if Jacob is riding around with those Jades, then he's just another one of Brandon's lackeys."

"Don't get yourself tangled," Poppy said when he saw the trouble that Libby was having with the foliage and terrain. "We're going to ..." he took a breath and looked around.

For a second, Libby saw his eye catch fire. The shadows masked his face, and she was in the presence of the soldier he'd always, under that grandfatherly exterior, been. Maybe he'd had his own plans all along.

"What we're going to do is find someplace to get you some medical attention, and I'm going to find a place to hide," Libby attempted to reason with him. "Not going back to the cottage — not until I find out what Brandon and Wilson are doing ... and you have a chance to explain to me how you know Jacob."

With her mention of Jacob again, another twist of doubt spiraled through Libby. *Were Brandon and Wilson the only threats? The real ones? Or were there more?*

She also had to wonder why Poppy kept wanting to stay close to her, and why he was the only one in town really who seemed to trust her with some of its secrets.

"I'll be fine. And—" Before Poppy could finish the sentence, Libby heard shouting.

"They know we've escaped," Libby said and pushed herself up. "We can't run through this jungle — I don't think they mow except for right next to the tracks. They'd see us in the open."

She thought some more. "Let me take you back to the library. I'm sure that they already checked in there once they saw that we had escaped. They would figure that we probably tried to get as far away from there as we could. That's why they are already out here looking for us. You can stay in there and I'll get help."

Poppy shook his head. "We can't split up. We're in this together. And you don't know the town like I do."

Libby frowned. "I'm not going back to town."

Poppy argued that they both needed a place to wait out the night, to catch their breath and clean up the mess escaping from Brandon and Wilson had left them in. Libby agreed to go with him back to the library and they made their way back through the thin ribbon of scrub that separated the railroad tracks from the library.

The silver BMW was in the parking lot, and Libby and Poppy could see lights bobbing along near the road. Poppy knew another way into the library, and he and Libby made their way in the dark to a small staff room on one of the upper floors.

Libby waited for what felt like several hours unable to do more than crouch near the door, listening. As far as she could tell, no one entered the library. Poppy's breathing evened out until she could hear him softly snoring, bivouacked in a corner between two chairs. She couldn't think straight.

Where could they go? She was going to be blamed for this. Brandon would make sure that

Atheneum ate her alive. It was obvious from the tunnels that the town had done that before, that at least some of the families — including the Sleuths — had decided that dividing up a small Texas town was not enough. Maybe they'd been skimming from the railroad before — maybe Brandon had been doing more than that now. After all, Texas wasn't the wild west. The library itself was a testament to the fact that they wanted some kind of connection to the rest of the world and the state, and the past was something worth preserving, regardless.

Preserving, but not acknowledging, perhaps. That determined her. Libby was going to go back to where it, where she, had started. She'd heard rumors of a graveyard on the old Sleuth property. It wasn't important enough for Brandon or Jacob to care about that lost little snippet of history. They probably didn't know or care that it was there. She was pretty sure that Brandon himself may have regarded tombstones as too much evidence to leave behind in most cases.

She opened the door slightly. The library was silent. She shut it again, leaned her body against it, locked it, and eventually fell asleep.

***

Poppy woke early enough to rile Libby just as the sky was beginning to lighten. She listened to their surroundings, and once she heard no other sounds, she carefully opened the door that she slept against to listen some more. When she was satisfied that she and Poppy were still alone, she snuck out to the snack machines to buy them breakfast with money that she found in a desk drawer. But Libby was no thief. She told herself that she would one day return the money with an explanation and an apology.

Poppy wasn't looking much better, and the chair bed he'd slept on seemed to have left him stiffer than she'd remembered seeing him the night before.

The bruises on both of them were much more prominent this morning, and as far as Libby was concerned, the public water fountain could have been coming straight from the headwaters of every magical spring she'd ever read about.

Stale donuts and water tightened her resolve to go out to the cemetery to see if she could figure out what was going on in this town. She could explore the land and see if there was something physical she could take away other than her and Poppy's injuries.

Poppy argued that she needed to wait with him, that what the town needed was to be made to face what Brandon was doing. "We need a chance to stand up to him."

Libby shook her head. "People have had a chance to stand up to him. They had a chance to ask for help, or to just keep being afraid. They chose fear."

"Don't think you can judge everyone at once." Poppy stood up. "We've had a long time to get rusty and sore doing things the way they've always been done. It's not just leap up and start running."

"I'm not asking for anyone to leap up," Libby reasoned. "Every back's been turned to me since the beginning. If anyone leapt up, it was to run in the other direction. And now here we are in the library looking like someone shook us hard out of a crime story. Jacob is with Brandon and Wilson, and I'm not ..."

Libby stopped. She wanted to say that all her trust was gone, but she did not want to bring up certain things to Poppy. He still had not told her how he knew Jacob. She wasn't going to her living family, and she wasn't going to run to strangers in some other town. She was going to the ones who tangled them into this town in the first place, and try to puzzle out what she remembered, and what Brandon was up to.

Poppy argued a little longer, but the effects of the past few days were beginning to show. Libby was sure that he'd be okay in the library, and that Daisy and the others would take care of him when they came in tomorrow. However anyone felt about Libby did not matter at this point. She knew they liked and respected Poppy, and he was clearly familiar with all the little routines and staff nooks. It was time for the two of them to separate, and she knew that he would be fine. Herself, she was not so sure.

A few minutes later, Libby was fast-walking from a side door out toward the garbage bins, around those into the little woods, and then toward the railroad track. She was pretty sure she knew which direction to go, but it was going to be a long walk.

Libby had just reached the tracks when Jacob stepped out of the trees, and for some reason did not startle her in the least.

"Thought you might have holed up in that library," he said. "I knew you would be smart enough to go back in there after we had already checked the whole building looking for you."

"Get away from me, Jacob," Libby said as she walked away from him.

"Listen to me!" Jacob followed her, talking as fast as he could. "I tried. Stayed near you, tried to be everything that you could have been. I was exhausted. You think it's easy working toward medical school, knowing that each test, each class, is just an opportunity to get chucked over? I met Brandon and he found out … I don't know how … who I was. He suggested real estate law, getting a place of my own, a place that didn't depend on shoving myself into some family that didn't really want me."

Libby kept walking. She could see his hands. She couldn't see his phone, though. For all she knew, Brandon had wired him up or something, and was following them, now.

"I don't care, Jacob." She turned around. She had to get him to leave.

The sun was rising over the trees and Jacob blinked as the light seemingly blinded him.

Libby kept talking. "Maybe I'll be sorry later, but I'm not going to listen to any more 'suggestions' or let anyone else try to define who I am because they don't like who *they* are."

"I like who I am just fine!" Jacob bellowed. "The real question is, do you have any idea what you're looking for, Libby? Think about what it would mean to find out that there is guilt that stretches back generations."

"What makes you think that I'm searching for anything?" Libby asked.

Jacob didn't answer that but said, "I have put off Brandon and Wilson for now. They do not want to bring any attention their way. They told me everything that Poppy said about them getting figured out too quickly if anything bad happened to either one of you. Go back to work tomorrow as normal, and don't give either one of them another thought."

"That sounds like a threat, Jacob." Libby glanced around for a large stick or a good place to run to.

"And what if it is?" he asked. "How many times do you think these trees have heard someone being told to leave well enough alone? The same warning over and over, and the same people over and over trying to make a little extra money and trying to gain a little more power? What do you want?"

He stopped to catch his breath but then kept going. "You're a mess. You've got the town's dirt in your blood, cousin. You willing to give some of that blood back? Pay it out in installments from someone else? How far are you willing to go? Who do you think you are!"

By now, the sun was up, striking her neck and shining full around her person. Jacob stood staring at her, his body as rigid as if he'd been turned to stone. Suddenly, he turned and stalked off. "Just you wait, little cousin. See you for lunch on Monday."

Libby watched him go, before cutting deeper into the woods, and kept walking.

***

Libby sank down to her knees. By now, there were grass stains on her legs, unidentifiable green and brown stains on her shoes. She couldn't quite catch her breath, all the words that she wanted to spit at Jacob wilting and dying in the back of her throat. Was that really why she'd been drawn to this place, insisted on going to the ball, stood up to Brandon? Because she believed Atheneum was a place worth the acts of violence?

There was a place here, a gravesite deep in the old property, that was the place where her bloodline started, started counting, all those years ago.

She pushed herself up. She didn't believe that the past was worth preserving if the vinegar that kept it fresh was Brandon Jade. She would yank every root up out of that ground.

She'd been walking for long enough. There had to be a road nearby or something. She wasn't going to think about the swift slither that had startled her several minutes ago. A small tree dragged a spiderweb through her hair as she brushed past it and then she saw them.

A small stone wall lay crumbled in a square around a small number of old gravestones and a slightly larger obelisk with the name Sleuth chiseled into it. Despite the obvious lack of any maintenance, the grass was low enough to see each headstone.

Libby walked up to the wall, paused, and then stepped into the square. Jacob's words echoed into her head. She was a Sleuth — these were her ancestors, and she'd been curious from the time she began to think about why she wasn't following her parents' expectations. Was there someone else back in the day whom she'd be able to point to? She would daydream herself into those ubiquitous DNA commercials. *My name is Libby and I'm not on the fast track to medical school, chasing my parents ... instead, I'm delving into the body of information, like my paternal great-grandmother, who was a brave lady reporter who tracked down an amazing story in California.*

    She'd never imagined standing in this graveyard, staring at these names. She was part of a family who'd founded a small town in Texas, which might be cool — a founding family sounded solid. But Jacob had been clear and Brandon's overreaction to her presence, to her poking around, to her friendship with Poppy — together these things let her know that it wasn't a happy story, the kind of story you'd read about in the pioneer tales section of the library.

    She knelt down, examining the closest stones and then working her way back along the rows, the men and women and children who made up the familial anchor for the Sleuth family in Atheneum. A beam of sunlight sparked in the grass behind one of the stones. Libby reached down for a stick, poking at the shine to make sure it wasn't something that bit or cut.

    Whatever it was flipped over. At first, she thought it might be a rusty can, then she realized it was a piece of jewelry. Dragging it up to the edge of the marker with the stick, she picked up what seemed to be a piece of a bracelet, maybe old enough to belong to the girl buried here. There were three charms attached to the chain, a star that might have come from a railroad inspector's badge, an acorn, and a key.

As Libby rubbed the metal, she realized it was a real key, attached with care to the broken chain. The star was a faded green, with a brassy sheen to its edges, while the acorn was black with tarnish. Perhaps it was silver? The key was a heavy one and the least damaged of the metal objects. Libby slid the chain into her pocket.

Would Poppy be able to give her some idea of what the key opened? Down in the tunnels, maybe, or wherever they kept the Barbecue Ball invitations. There were secrets in this town that Libby was going to have out in the light of day. Her memories and her family and who she was could squirm all they wanted, there would be a reckoning and sunlight right in the heart of these shadows.

Was Poppy okay? Libby cringed. She'd left him, injured, at the edge of town. And she'd been angry — he knew more than he was telling her, and she'd treated him like he was just another one of the townspeople she'd encountered. Maybe he'd forgive her if she got back. *If* she could make it to him before Brandon did.

Jacob, though ... he'd been headed that way. Would she have a chance to get to Poppy again, in private so that no one would know about the key?

She turned around and began stomping back through the trees, swallowing an urge to start yelling. She couldn't be far from someplace. Atheneum wasn't that big.

She heard a buzz and a rumble and realized that someone was coming through the trees on three-wheelers or motorbikes. Her throat closed. She balled her fist around the metal in her pocket and headed away from the trail she'd been following, going away from the sound as best she could.

The sun speared each open area. Her head pounded. She paused for a minute, near to a thick pine trunk. She closed her eyes as her throat pulsed and lights sparked behind her eyes.

Darkness shoved her elsewhere.

Chapter Twelve
by Jesus Galvan

Jane!

Libby thought about her, and garnered hope that she could probably help her. Libby had been planning to go back for more psychic readings, but she had not done so thus far. She reasoned that no one would think to look for her there.

It only took ten minutes to walk to Jane's house from the Sleuth land. Now that Libby had to hide within wooded areas all weekend, she felt that she really knew Atheneum now. Not to mention the underground tunnels. That was Atheneum inside and out. Literally inside the earth.

She reached Jane's house from her backyard by climbing a fence. Libby looked down at her skirt and blouse and confirmed that they were filthy. She tried to remember what made her choose those items on a day that she was not going to work. Not that she could have in any way imagined that what happened to her in the past two days was going to transpire, and that she could have worn clothes better suited for the ordeal. After her agony, she knew that she would probably burn these clothes and remove the physical evidence of this day.

What attempt Libby made in the bathroom at the library this morning to make herself look better was gone. Her hair was unkempt again. Still she used her hands to try to smooth it down. She thought it would be worse to turn on Jane's outside spigot and get water to clean her face. She didn't know what Jane would think about that. She would just explain to Jane as best she could as to why she has shown up on her doorstep looking the way that she does.

She knocked on Jane's back door, and right away came a very familiar voice.

"It's about time you showed up. We've got a lot to do to get our stories straight," Brandon bellowed before forcefully opening the door. The utter shock on his face matched Libby's when he saw her standing there before him.

"You've got to be kidding me," they both said in unison.

Jane bounded to the door and joined the shock. "Uh-oh."

"Are you following me, Brandon?" Libby asked.

"Ummmmm ... Looks like I was here first," Brandon replied sarcastically. "I won't even tell you all of the other things wrong with your question." He sounded very calm, and that was disturbing to Libby after all that she had encountered from him this weekend.

"You two need to stop it," Jane intervened. "This whole situation is an utter mess. Libby come inside before someone sees you." Jane was incredibly calm and seemed to already know what took place.

"What is going on?" Libby asked without making an attempt to go into the house. "How do you just "happen" to be at the person's house that I just "happened" to come to? Did you insert a microchip or some kind of tracker in me?" Libby asked and then thought, *this town has not failed in being strange and insane.*

Libby was hesitant. She had no idea why Brandon was here. She did not know what would happen once she got inside of Jane's house. Brandon seemed to read her thoughts. "Do you think us Jades would let some freak show like this live in this town if she wasn't related? She's an utter embarrassment."

"That's why I stay. Just to get on the family's nerves. I know I would be much happier somewhere else," Jane said.

Jane must have noticed the confused look on Libby's face, and could sense her hesitance. "Oh, yeah. You don't know," she said while shaking her head.

"Let me explain," Jane said before taking a deep breath. "Brandon and Wilson are my brothers. Brandon came here tonight and told me everything. He thought that I could somehow predict exactly what was going to happen to him after what he has done to you and Grant," Jane said, calling Poppy by his real name.

Jane looked at Brandon and continued, "This wonderful guy here knows that he has really messed up this time. He apparently did not think anything through. I don't even know what he thought he was going to gain," Jane continued.

She rolled her eyes at her brother before turning back to look at Libby again. "This is pure nonsense. Year after year, from his mouth is Sleuth Sleuth Sleuth, and their property that he cannot get his hands on. I don't know why it is so important to him. He acts like there is still oil in the land, which there hasn't been since eighty-eight."

Jane huffed, took a pause, then looked at Brandon again. "We Jades already own plenty of land here and in Gheldoux. What are you even going to do with that Sleuth dirt and weeds, Brandon?"

"Maybe we want to give it to you," he answered."

Jane knew right away that he was being dishonest, and her neutral facial expression showed that to Brandon.

"Fine. Don't believe me," he said with the same aloofness that Jane showed.

"Anyway, back to the situation at hand," Jane focused back on Libby. "Brandon was telling me that he knows that he has to leave you alone, and he hopes that you will agree to say nothing. This would be a weird situation to explain to the police. Where would you even start Libby?"

That was a good point. Even if she filed charges, would the police handle her case properly? Were there Jades on the force or in the prosecution? Could she take the case to another town to avoid the potential bias? There was too much to ponder in this short period of time.

Jane interrupted Libby's thoughts. "Bonnie is probably making the rounds looking for Brandon. I'm sure that Grant told her who had him looking like he did. Brandon still has to figure out what he is going to say to her."

Brandon cleared his throat and started buffing the fingernails on his left hand with his right thumb.

"After a shower and a fresh change of clothes, you will be as good as new," Jane told

Libby. "I can take you home, and all will be fine from here on out. Right, Brandon?"

"Yeah, yeah. I promise to leave you alone, Libby," he said, using the voice of an indifferent child that is apologizing only because they are being forced to.

Jane stuck her head out of the door and looked to Libby's left and right. "I wish you would just come inside. I do not feel comfortable talking to you like this."

Libby knew that it was risky to go into the house, as well as have Jane give her a ride home. But at this point, she did not know what else she had to lose. Every move she made, even if she was alone would be risky.

"I will not say anything, but what about Bonnie?" Libby asked.

Brandon cleared his throat again and walked away.

Jane's face filled with fear as she looked in Brandon's direction. "What do you mean by that?" Jane turned back around and asked Libby.

"Well that's a dumb question," Libby felt like she could be as surly as she wanted although there was still the possibility of more brutality from Brandon or Wilson. "Poppy has numerous bruises on his face alone. I'm sure there's more on the rest of his body. How do you propose Poppy will get out of telling Bonnie what happened to him?"

"Oh," Jane laughed nervously. "That's what you meant. Of course." She looked at Brandon again as he walked back toward the two women.

"Just worry about yourself, Libby. Don't concern yourself with other people's problems," Brandon said.

"Other people's problems?" Libby used her hands to stretch out her shirt and skirt. "After what you have put me through in the past two days, I believe this is also *my* problem!"

"Whatever," he said, his tone indifferent again. "And oh, yeah. Here's your stuff." He reached into his front pants and pulled out Libby's cell phone and slim billfold.

Libby snatched the items out of Brandon's hand and then made a fake lunge at him. "I just wanna—"

"We can't stay here in this doorway and keep this up," Jane interrupted. She grabbed her keys from a nearby counter and told Libby to meet her in the front yard at her car.

Once Libby was there, she sank down into the passenger seat. Her body was receiving a little bit of comfort, but that was it. Her mind was still worried about Jane's plans and intentions.

"I am trying to wrap my head around the fact that you are Wilson and Brandon's sister," Libby said to Jane once they had reached Libby's driveway. The two had not said anything else to each other during the ride. "Why didn't you tell me that before?"

"It wasn't really something that came up during our interactions," Jane reasoned.

"Even when I said that I worked at HouBayou? The place where one of your brothers works, and your other brother always seems to be? I'm scared to find out what else is not worth mentioning," Libby said and exited the car.

Libby waited for 10 minutes after Jane left her driveway. Then she started packing some clothes, as she had already decided that she was going to spend the night in a hotel. She added plenty of extras to her suitcase, and included toiletries. She brushed her hair and changed into some clean clothes, but she did not take a shower. She was already apprehensive about being in the house alone. With water running, she would be in a more vulnerable position because she would be unable to hear noises to indicate that someone had entered her house. She would take a shower at the hotel.

She lifted and moved the foot of her bed askew about two feet. She lifted back part of the rug that was there and lifted up some floorboards. There contained a medium sized safe. In the safe was three thousand dollars in cash that Libby kept there in case of an emergency. Right now was such a time. There was also the key to a safe deposit box at a bank in Tomball.

***

Libby entered the parking garage of the Jardin del Verde hotel on Baker Road in Tomball. She had checked her rearview mirror several times the whole way from her house to the hotel to see if she was being followed, and she planned to completely check her surroundings once she got herself and her suitcase out of the car. She was glad that there were plenty of empty spaces on the ground floor of the garage, because she did not want to have to use a stairwell or an elevator.

She felt like her neck had turned into a swivel after turning it back so many times on her way to the lobby. She breathed a sigh of relief once she reached the front desk. Still, she looked around at all the faces of everyone around before she fully approached the counter.

"May I help you, Señora?" a young, dark-haired man behind the counter asked.

When Libby continued to keep looking around, he said, "Miss? Are you looking for someone?"

Libby looked at him and realized she should probably look less apprehensive. If she were to look distressed or agitated, the desk clerk may be hesitant to rent her a room.

She stepped over and mustered up as much of a smile as she could before telling him, "I'd like to rent a suite for the night, please."

"Yes, of course, Señora. Will it be for just yourself, or do you need a double-occupancy room?" he asked before typing into his computer.

Libby informed him that it was just for her, and the two of them discussed the options and amenities. She had expected to pay a hefty deposit since she wasn't using a credit card, and she was glad that the clerk accepted cash from her without a hassle.

Once she finished the transaction and had her key card, she went to the vending machines that she saw in the lounge. The desk clerk had already informed her that the hotel restaurant was already closed, and that she could only order room service if she was using a credit card to rent the room. Her ordeal during the past two days kept food far from her mind. Now that she felt a little safer, she had full realization of how famished she was. This was going to be Libby's second meal of the day that came from a vending machine, but she planned to treat it like it was lobster and Beef Wellington.

While she pondered her choices, she heard someone behind her say, "Trains still have not run on that line since Friday night. And Essex-Knight released a statement today saying that they are not sure when operations will be back to normal."

She looked over at the man that she figured had been talking. He was sitting with a woman on a large sofa, of whom asked, "Why not?"

He said, "They are not done with their investigation of the car on the tracks that got hit. When first-responders got to the car, it was on fire. At first it was assumed that the impact of the train started the fire. But after they interviewed the operator of the train, he said that he could see that there were flames inside the car before it got hit.

"From his window when he was about 30 seconds away, all of a sudden the car appeared on the tracks and stopped. Of course there was no way for him to stop in time. When they went back to that train intersection for the investigation, they found spike strips close by. They believe that they were deliberately placed there so that the car would get stuck on the tracks. And there was a small decline at that intersection. They believe that one was specifically chosen so that the car could easily be pushed down at the right time. The train operator, however, says that he only saw the car as it came onto the tracks, and did not see any figures running away from the car."

"Do they know whose car it was?" the woman asked.

"Yeah. Her name is Bonnie. She lives or lived there in Atheneum," the man answered.

"What do you mean by that?"

"None of the investigators are saying anything about her as far as if she was in the car or not."

Libby gasped loud enough for the two people to look over at her.

"Something happened to Bonnie?" she asked the man, walking over closer to him.

"Ummmm ... Do we know you, Ma'am?" the woman asked Libby, giving her a venomous look.

Libby was wise enough to know this meant that she was not getting an answer to her question. She grabbed her suitcase and went to her room without getting anything from the vending machine.

***

On her way to HouBayou the next morning, Libby stopped at Denovo Coffee for some expresso. After hearing about Bonnie, it had been hard for Libby to fall asleep the night before, and she was extremely drowsy.

On the advice of Jane, she went to her work area and put on the façade of everything being business as usual. She did not see Wilson there at any point during the morning, and that helped the situation. She concentrated on making a plan of getting caught up on work after her long time away. While doing that, she was still able to note that she did not hear any conversations about Bonnie or the train situation.

During her lunch time, she followed through with her plans to go to the bank and access her safety deposit box. Once inside the vault, she examined the contents and started mentally making plans of what her next moves should be.

There was banking information for the funds from the cryptocurrency investment. It was a different bank than where she had decided to open an account and get a safe deposit box when she had first moved to Atheneum. There was also a jiffy envelope with a letter detailing the instructions of steps she needed to take at the time. She had not received these items at the same time. One afternoon in February, during her graduating semester in college, Jacob's friend came to her dorm with the banking information. A week later, the letter was slipped under her door.

She stood in the vault and read an excerpt from the letter:

It is understood that it was an innocent mistake for you to have uncovered this information about the Sleuths. All will be fine as long as you say nothing to anyone about what you now know.

You must leave the area. It is unfortunate that you will not be able to finish your studies. We have a job arranged for you in the town in which you will be moving. Although you have money enough to pay your moving expenses, we will still finance that for you.

You should start packing your most beloved items now, but do not bring attention to yourself. Bring your items to be stored in your car a little at a time on a daily basis. Do not attempt to take everything. At most you should only be focusing on your clothing and toiletries. At a moment's notice, you will need to able to get the last of your belongings out of your room quickly, and begin your journey. On that day, you will receive further instructions of where to pick up your cash for your move.

Libby focused in greater detail on the part that said, *"You have money enough to pay your moving expenses."*

She thought back to what Jacob said about it being unrealistic that Libby could have made a lot of money from her investment as quickly as she had. When she read the letter two years ago, she assumed that it was referring to the very comfortable lifestyle that her parents had always afforded her. Now she wasn't sure if it instead referred to the cryptocurrency money.

But since she had already received the bank information about the investment money, why was she given more money for moving? Were these aspects related, or were there separate, unrelated forces that wanted her out of Louisiana?

Chapter Thirteen
by Alpana Sarangapani

Libby came out of the bank and got into her car. Her stomach was grumbling, and there was a dull feeling of pain in her head. She was famished. Even though she had not counted on her vending machine dinner plans to be interrupted the night before, she was still to blame for trying to survive off of just coffee that morning. She would not be able to fully concentrate on her thoughts and questions until she got some nutrients into her body. What she just retrieved from the bank was too crucial to graze over.

There was flexibility in the working hours at HouBayou, so Libby would be able to justify her absence and modify her work time as needed. This was just the time for that, as she was not going to be able to get back to the office anytime soon if she wanted to get a good meal. At the same time, she really did not care. A few days ago, she had been thinking about leaving the job, so if she was reprimanded at this point, so be it. After her weekend ordeal, she had not even known if she was going to make it back to work or anywhere else for that matter. So right now, Libby was going to make food a priority.

After a fast-food meal that she ravaged through, she went back to work, and stayed until 4 p.m. The afternoon was the same as the morning. Everything was business as usual, and neither Wilson nor Angela were there throughout the rest of Libby's day. She was glad that she had also not had to deal with Brandon at all that day.

She had already paid for tonight, but she decided that she would extend her stay at the hotel for few more days beyond that. She was not in a state to go back to her house yet, she just did not feel safe.

After making the arrangements at the front desk, she knew that she needed some food to have in her hotel room. Although she needed something quick at the time, Libby had been feeling guilty after her fast-food lunch. She decided she should buy some fruits to have in her room. This was after she had been missing eating fresh fruits as much as she would have liked in the last few weeks. She had been trying to eat healthy for last two years and had been doing a good job at it. While she had been in college, healthy eating wasn't something she could even conceive with her workload. Now that it was a priority, she did not want to ruin her wise habits after a few bad weeks.

As there was a supermarket just a few blocks from the hotel, Libby decided to walk down to the store. She saw an abundance of clouds in the sky and knew that it might rain fairly soon, but she hoped that it wouldn't.

Once at the store and browsing the produce section, Libby saw Captain Smith of the local police department. She had seen him on duty on many occasions, including at the Barbecue Ball that she attended a few weeks ago. Before that she had also heard of him in conversations at work but had never been introduced to him.

She had neglected to take a shopping cart and tried to carry the fruits in her hand. She could hardly manage to walk to the cashier's station that had a long line of people. She stood in line with much difficulty. That's when she saw Captain Smith coming to the same line in which she was standing. He had all kinds of foods in his cart.

"Do you want to put your stuff in my cart," he asked, seeing her trying to manage to stop them from falling.

"No, thank you, I will be fine," she said politely.

Libby had only two people in front of her, one of which was a woman almost done paying for her stuff but was just told by the cashier that she was short by five cents. Libby wished she had her hands free to could give it to the lady, and let the line go forward. *I surely know I have a nickel in my purse*, she thought immediately, so she could start putting her stuff on the counter after the lady was gone.

The man in front of her put the divider bar at the end of his stuff that he put on the conveyor. As she was feeling relieved and started to put her stuff on the conveyor belt, suddenly one of the kiwifruit from a bag popped out and fell on the floor. While trying to pick it up, she dropped all the rest of them from that bag.

"Allow me to help, please!" she heard Captain Smith again. He started helping her pick up each one of the kiwis to put on the conveyor belt. She could not refuse this time, and she obliged and thanked him.

Finally, it was her turn to pay for her items. She also bought two reusable cloth bags from the store so she could carry her groceries easily while walking back to the hotel. She paid the amount due with her debit card, nodded to Captain Smith and left the store. All the time that she had been hoping for it not to rain went in vain. It was pouring down now.

"Oh, no!" she sighed and sat on the bench that was there right outside the front door of the store. Luckily for her, that area was protected from the rain, so she decided to wait there until the rain stopped.

"It wasn't going to rain today, according to the weather forecast for the day," a voice came from behind her. She turned her head and saw Captain Smith who was just coming out of the store.

"Oh, yes! That's what I too saw when I started the day this morning!" she said. She had turned on the news that morning while getting ready for work, hoping to hear something about Bonnie or the train crash.

"I'm Captain Joshua Smith, by the way. I am with the police department of the city of Atheneum," he replied. "I guess I should formally introduce myself at this point."

"That goes for me as well," Libby said. "I'm Libby. Libby Ferguson. I am with HouBayou Publishing. Nice to meet you."

"Ah, Ms. Ferguson, I've heard of you a lot from Poppy, and finally it is nice to meet you today." He extended his right hand to shake hands with her.

What a nice and friendly person he is, she thought, remembering the unfriendly behavior of the people in her office and the town. All except for Poppy, Ruthie, and Jane.

"I also saw you a few times in Atheneum, one time in particular was during the ball, Captain Smith," she said.

"So, how do you like it there? A beautiful and peaceful place to live with an equally beautiful community of friendly people, isn't it?" Captain Smith asked. He sounded so proud of his community.

Libby thought to herself: *I can't say everyone is friendly after what I have been seeing during my two years here!* But she kept a friendly face, so Captain Smith wouldn't know what she was thinking.

"Yes, indeed, it is a beautiful place. I am still kind of new here, so am still trying to meet and know the people," she answered.

"So you're in the publishing business. Have you ever published or thought of writing something of your own?" Captain Smith asked.

"No, I haven't published anything yet, though I'm thinking of writing a novel — based on some historical events," she blurted out and surprised herself. She realized how quickly she told him about her secret desire to go on to become a fiction writer herself, at some point of her life. She had not revealed that to anyone since she started working in the business.

"Ah, that is interesting! Are you thinking of including something about our little town in there?" Captain Smith asked her.

"Perhaps!" she replied, getting a little annoyed at herself for talking about her plans about writing to a complete stranger.

She looked towards the parking lot and saw that most of the rain had let up.

"Oh, the rain has stopped. I have to go. It was very nice to have met you, Captain. Smith. I will see you around," she said and stood up to gather her bags.

"Oh, yes. It was nice to have met you too, Ms. Ferguson. Why don't you put your bags in my cart instead of carrying all the way to your car?" he asked, trying to make some room in his cart.

"No, thank you. I am fine. My hotel is just a few streets down, so I didn't bring my car," she said it in one single breath and surprised herself again for talking and telling him so much about herself.

"It is still drizzling, and it won't be dry and nice to walk, even if the hotel is only a few blocks from here. I'd like to give you a ride if you don't mind, Ms. Ferguson," he said politely.

Even though they just met, she had seen him working with people on various occasions, and after all, he is a police officer. She felt safe and started thinking that maybe she should just accept his offer as she'd be all wet by the time she got to her hotel even though it was only drizzling.

Libby agreed and told him, "Okay, I think you are right, Captain Smith. This rain is still good enough to get all wet if one is walking for even a short distance. I accept your kind offer of giving me a ride. Thank you."

"You're most welcome," he said and helped her to put her two bags in his cart. They walked to his car, a black Chevy Camaro, parked on the left side of the building. He opened the front-side passenger door to allow her to sit down. He put her bags on the rear seat first, so she would be able to quickly pick them up and leave when they got to the hotel. He then loaded the trunk with his groceries, put the cart back into the cart-deposit slot of the parking lot, came back and got into the driver's seat.

"Are you okay, Ms. Ferguson?" he asked.

"I am fine. Thank you again for giving me a ride," she replied, and he started driving.

Even with the wait on the blinking traffic lights that were malfunctioning due to the rain and the wind, they entered the hotel driveway in less than five minutes. He pulled over to the porte-cochère of the hotel and stopped right in front of the main entrance, so she wouldn't have to walk far as it was still drizzling. He put the car in park and got out to help her to get her bags out, but she promptly got out, opened the back door herself and took out the bags. One of the attendants of the hotel came forward to help, but she waved him away, thanking him.

"Thank you so much again, Captain Smith. That was very kind of you. Hope to see you around." Libby told him.

"Oh, not a problem, Ms. Ferguson. Please give me a call anytime you need something, or just a friend or someone to talk to," he blurted out. He opened his wallet to take out a business card. He gave it to her saying, "Here is my card with my contact information. And again, please do not hesitate to call me if you need anything, anytime."

"Sure, Captain Smith. I will do that. Thank you," Libby said, raised her hand to say goodbye to him, and placed the card in her purse.

Captain Smith looked into her eyes and said, "I'm sorry. There is just one request I do have to ask."

Libby didn't say anything. She just stared back at him and hoped he would say it without her giving permission.

"Please. Call me Joshua," he said, and then walked back to his car and drove away.

Libby took the elevator to her room on the 3rd floor. She opened the door, got inside her room, and put the bags on the table. Then she went straight to the bathroom to wipe and dry her hair that had got a little wet while walking to Captain Smith's car. She came out and plugged in the coffee pot to boil some water to make a cup of green tea. She was glad that she bought some cookies that she has always liked to have with black or green tea. She looked at the clock, and it was past 6 o'clock already.

She sat down by the glass window that gave her a view of a big part of both Baker and Main Streets there in Tomball. She loved the scene — seeing people walking, and driving in a slower mode in the evening, was putting her in a relaxed mood. She could also see the colorful garden in the hotel courtyard and was enjoying that as well.

The water started boiling, and she grabbed a mug from the cabinet. After cleaning and rinsing it, she poured the water in, and dropped in the tea bag to steep. She opened her shopping bags and emptied out her items. She nicely arranged the items on shelves and in the mini fridge. She took two oatmeal coconut cookies and washed one of the small, ripe nectarines to eat for the time being.

She then got one of the books that she borrowed from the library, grabbed her food and drink, and went back to sit at the window. Like Poppy's, this book had historical facts about Atheneum. It surprised her to find quite a few books in the library that were written about the small town, but they only seemed to contain boring data and numbers. They were merely text facts. Poppy's book was the only one that had pictures and fun details.

Looking out again, she felt relaxed after taking a few sips of the tea, and a bite on one of the cookies. "Heavenly!" she said at a volume that could almost be a scream. She opened to the page where her bookmark was. Reading these non-fiction books about the history of the town was what presently got her into thinking of writing a fiction book based on her experiences of the last two years in Atheneum. She imagined that the protagonist of her future book could be a woman who grew up in a similar town without knowing any of the dark secrets it held, and but was determined to get to the bottom of it when she started learning about some things that had been closeted.

    She decided that she would go to the museum on Monday, during her lunch break. The museum was just a few blocks away from her office. It might have some information of the old families with pictures that would help her to write a book embedded with facts, but passed off as fiction.

    Within a few chapters, she finished the cookies, her tea, and the nectarine too. She paused from her reading and started to think about the incident of meeting with Captain Smith. She tried to shake off her thoughts, but could not help thinking about him. He had been so very considerate, friendly, and respectful to her so close to the town that is filled with so many unfriendly, rather rude people that do not hesitate to not just ignore her, but also heap insults.

    Libby wasn't able to reach her purse on the bed without getting up, so she went there and laid on her side. She took out Captain Smith's card and smoothed her index finger over the shiny embossing. While they had been in the store, she pretended not to notice when he had mentioned Poppy. She thought back to what he said, *"I've heard of you a lot from Poppy."*

She didn't know how to take that. Were they good, innocent things, or bad things? What reason did Poppy have to be speaking to Captain Smith about Libby? While ruminating over this, the plot for her book, and her plans to collect materials for it to start, she drifted off to sleep.

***

Libby woke up to knocking on her hotel door. She lay still, and slowly gained her composure. She wondered why someone would be knocking at her room door, and realized that it would be best for her not to answer.

"Room Service, Ma'am," a female voice from the hallway said. "Do you need to order anything for dinner?"

Libby looked at the clock on the bedside table. It was past 8 o'clock already. "No, thank you," she answered through the door. "I will go downstairs to the restaurant and have my dinner there. Thank you, though!"

"Very well, Ma'am. Have a nice evening," the woman said.

Libby first went to thinking that she liked the way the hotel operated there, and that they were providing excellent customer service with a personal touch to all their customers.

Yet instead, Libby felt that something wasn't right. She knew that usually you have to order Room Service for them to show up at your door, and they do not just randomly knock on doors and ask guests. On top of that, Libby had already been told that she could not order from Room Service because she had not used a credit card for her stay.

Now she wished that she had told the woman that she would stay in her room because she already had food there. Libby was apprehensive about leaving the room now, and she remained in the bed and dwelled on it for several more minutes. She finally decided that she would go down to the restaurant, but she would wait until she heard other voices in the hallway and go downstairs only if someone else was riding down the elevator with her.

She got up and wanted to get refreshed and changed for dinner before it got too late, but there was something else that she wanted to do before that. She got her cell phone and dialed a number on the keypad.

"Captain Smith?" she asked when she got an answer. "This is Libby Ferguson." She pressed the speakerphone function to make sure that she could hear him best. Libby heard a harumph from his end.

"I'm sorry," she said. "Joshua."

"That's better," he said. "And to what do I owe the pleasure of getting a call from you this soon? Not that I mind at all," he added a chuckle at the end.

"I-I, um, didn't expect to use your number so soon either ... if at all," Libby stammered, feeling flushed. "But I do sort of need ... I mean, umm ... I guess it's best to say that I am looking for some information about someone."

"I see," Captain Smith replied. Once Libby didn't say anything else for the next few moments, he asked, "Are you asking me to run a check on someone?"

Libby said, "No. Nothing like that."

"That's good," he said. "I would have hated to have to tell you no."

"The person I'm asking about is Poppy."

"I can see if I can help you out. I guess it depends on what you want to know."

"I'm concerned about his whereabouts. I was expecting to see him earlier today, but he didn't show up," Libby lied.

"Oh. That's an easy one to answer. He's in the hospital."

"What? Why?" Libby practically yelled. She wondered if Brandon or Wilson had gone back and discovered Poppy in the library and done him worse. Jacob may have spilled the beans about Poppy's whereabouts after he saw Libby in the woods on Sunday morning. She thought that he was fine enough when she left him, and that he would give some plausible explanation to the library staff the next day as to why he was there. She thought maybe he could even find somewhere to remain stowed until the building opened, then come out undetected and mingle in among the other library patrons.

"I just know about this because I was at the hospital at the time on some other business," Captain Smith said. "It suddenly got busy and very animated in the emergency room. I think mainly because of who the patient was. Poppy is a very well-known character around town. Several doctors and nurses stayed among the area and situation.

"One of the paramedics that bought him in said that personnel of the library had found him near the back door of a storage room, and that hardly anybody uses that particular one. It was only by chance that an employee had gone into that storage to pick up the signs for a big once-a-year event that they were preparing for. He heard soft moaning and some rustling, and saw Poppy struggling to sit upright, with his back against the wall.

"He was extremely weak, dehydrated, and disoriented when they found him. The EMT personnel made his condition somewhat stable, and took him to the hospital," Captain Smith finished.

"How is he now? Did you get to talk to him, and find out what happened to him?" Libby asked, trying to stay resolute in thinking that she made the right decision to leave Poppy at the library where he could be safe. She was determined to ward off any guilt that might creep up.

"He is in much better condition now," Captain Smith said. "All he can remember was that he had been tied up and kept in a closed room somewhere, but he could not remember how he got to the library in that state.

"I told him to focus on getting well, and to take his time in remembering things. I assured him that we would get to the bottom of this in due time. In my city, nobody gets away with any kind of criminal behavior," declared Captain Smith.

Libby was happy that she had finally met someone in Atheneum that was being nice to her, and Captain Smith appeared to be genuine in his kindness. But after her ordeal with Brandon and Wilson over the weekend, she wasn't sure if his last declaration was a little short-sighted.

Chapter Fourteen
by Christina Gray

The hotel dining room was already crowded when she walked into the beautifully appointed room. Silver and gold sparkled on every table filled with smartly dressed patrons which caused Libby to look down uncertainly at her plain skirt and blouse. She would have to grab something nicer from the area clothing stores, most of which, she noticed on her last outing were within walking distance.

Libby felt exposed standing in the entrance, and she scanned the room dreading to see any familiar faces. She breathed a sigh of relief when she didn't see anyone she knew. She approached the hostess to be seated.

"Excuse me ma'am." Libby instinctively kept her voice low so that it wouldn't carry across the softly buzzing room.

The hosted looked pretty but bored. "Name? How many in your party?" Her tone belied the courteous words as she didn't appear to really care what the answer would be. That is until it came.

"Libby Ferguson. I'm staying in the hotel and was told I could dine here." The young girl's once dull eyes began to sparkle and shine and the smile on her face became wide and sincere.

"Ms. Ferguson, we have been expecting you." Confusion and fear warred on her face. *Had someone found her so quickly? And if so, who? Had Brandon decided to go back on his word to Jane and make good on his earlier promises delivered in the bowels of the library?* A shudder ran though her that was missed by the girl who stood across from her.

The now perky hostess grabbed a menu and a set of cloth-covered silverware and moved deeper into the dining room. She had not noticed that her guest had not followed her and stood trembling at the podium.

Libby's stomach rolled and pitched. On knees newly-jellied, she slowly moved to follow the retreating figure. *What lay at the end of this? Or more appropriately who? Could Brandon actually get away with kidnapping her in front of all of these people the way he did at the library?* This wasn't Atheneum, after all.

Before she reached the table, Libby decided that she would make a big enough scene that they would either leave, or the police would be called. *She would be safe in jail from them, right?* She was so caught up in her thoughts that she almost bumped into the hostess who had come to an abrupt stop.

Her eyes flew up from the expensive flooring and landed on her dinner companions. Shock sent a cold wave crashing through her body and glued her mouth shut. The eyes that regarded her were familiar, but instead of the anger and hostility that she would have expected to see, she found they silently begged for understanding and forgiveness. They were eyes that belonged to her mother and father.

Libby closed her own eyes, sure that this was another dream, and that when she opened them she would be sitting on her own bed petting Greystoke, or perhaps still standing at the entrance and scanning the room. Perhaps her stress had created this dream.

When she opened them again, her mother, face unlike her own, and father still sat at the nicely appointed table. *Obviously not a dream*, she thought to herself. The hostess had deposited the menu and silverware, delicately snatched a hundred-dollar-bill from between the fingers of Libby's father, and then quickly escaped the tense atmosphere.

Although her parents were at a corner table that had no one else seated nearby, Libby felt that she might be drawing unwanted attention by standing and staring somewhat stupidly at her parents.

She sat down gingerly on the edge of her chair, eyes down, keeping her back stiff as she remembered their last meeting. They too must have been reliving it as well, because tears slid down her mother's perfectly made up face, and her father's hand reached across the table and captured one of her own. She instinctively tried to pull away, but he held on firmly until she looked up and into his eyes. They looked tortured, and she found herself relaxing in his grip.

No one spoke for a bit, and a smartly dressed waiter appeared to take their order. Libby hadn't opened her menu yet and was grudgingly appreciative when her father ordered for them all. Libby listened to the cadence of his deep voice and memories of his love slid through her. She had missed him terribly.

Libby furrowed her brow when she looked at her mother to his right. No such memories existed with her.

It was her father, as always, who broke the silence. "Please let us explain everything — our reaction when you showed up unexpectedly, the reason we so badly handled your genealogy project the way we did, and our disappointment about you not following in the family business. Even about your disappearance." His voice was pleading.

"We were afraid," her mother cut in. "To be perfectly honest, we still are." Her face showed the fear just below the surface, and twin tracks through her mother's expensive make up. How had she never noticed that her mother was beautiful even when she cried?

"Why couldn't you just leave well enough alone?" her mother's voice was noticeably quieter when she said that, but then rose again. "Jacob was supposed to watch over you. We paid him well enough to—"

"Enough!" Libby's father cut her off. His voice was uncharacteristically sharp with his beloved wife. She looked startled and fell obediently silent.

"Enough," he said again, in a lowered voice. He looked around uncomfortably, making sure that there was still no one else within earshot of their conversation.

"When we heard you were doing a genealogy project, we knew already what you would find," he explained. "Your mother told me about the rumors in her family when we first met. The ones they whispered thinking no one was listening. We decided to keep it from you both for your own safety. We had money enough that you need never worry about any other family. When you began that project, we were afraid it would bring trouble to our doorstep. We encouraged Jacob to distract you and put an end to the project, and persuade you not to turn it in. But he failed. He has always just been an annoying failure that we had to put up with."

Her mother's mouth stiffened, and she glowered at Libby's father. "Perhaps that should be a story for another day."

Her father cleared his throat and looked back at Libby. "When you dropped out of school and disappeared, we were afraid that you had been hurt. All kinds of thoughts floated through our minds at first. Then you started calling the house and our cell phones, and we were relieved that you were okay. Still, we thought it was safer not to answer, so that there was no connection on the line that could be traced. Once we found out from Richie that you were actually speaking on the phone and texting each other, we had to get rid of that line. We didn't want you to be tracked. We aren't proud of our actions, but people with no conscience were looking for your mother as sole surviving heir and would have no problem using you to get to her. The Jade family is very powerful here in Texas."

"The Jade family is evil," Libby whispered hotly across the table. At that moment, two servers arrived with their food, and the three of them remained quiet while the plates were put before them. Libby kept her eyes averted away from her parents' faces, still feeling discomforted by their sudden presence in town. Libby had lost her appetite and knew she would probably just push her food around with her fork, while her parents ate.

After the servers left, Libby began telling her parents about her move to Atheneum, and what has happened in her life for the past two years. At the first mention of her job at HouBayou, her father looked startled, but said nothing. Her mother's face paled and her fork stilled. Libby didn't bother to indicate her start as a contract employee.

She didn't pull any punches when she told her parents about how the townspeople treated her, but she beamed when she talked about Poppy and Ruthie.

Outwardly, she forced herself to have only happy thoughts and words about Poppy. But during the midst of the conversation, it was impossible not to think about Poppy's current state.

"Well it certainly seems like you're happy here, and doing well at your job," her mother said. "You have always loved reading. It seems like a perfect career for you."

Libby was stunned. She could not understand how her mother interpreted the description of her life for the past two years as being pleasant. She had included that she had only met Poppy and Ruthie a month ago, and that shouldn't have qualified in anyone's mind that she was all of a sudden blissful in Atheneum. Maybe it would take nothing short of giving her parents all of the details about her and Poppy's kidnapping in order for them to ask her to come back home. It was creeping into her head that her parents wanted her to stay here in harm's way.

Libby just looked down at her plate and blinked back her tears. Her voice shook when she said, "Yeah. Everything is perfect."

A server approached their table and asked to take their plates. He raised an eyebrow at the amount of food still on Libby's plate, and asked her if she wanted it boxed up. She looked up at him, and then declined his offer.

She looked at her father after that, hoping that he would see the pleading in her eyes, and express his love to her, as he always did when she was growing up.

He looked at her, and a smile slowly formed on his face. He rubbed his hands together, and then asked the server, "What desserts do you have here?"

Libby faintly heard him order key lime pie after the waiter rattled off the options. Her head plopped on the table in front of her, and the visions started forming. *Aunt Melanie. Snow. Roller coaster. Mom.*

Although they were barely audible, this time there were voices with the dream.

"Get her Nathaniel, before she goes too far under. Give her the inhalant before she starts remembering."

Mom. Waves. Airplane. Aunt Melanie.

"Is she all right?"

"Yes. She's fine. She sometimes gets lightheaded if she waits too long to eat."

"But she's definitely okay. No need to worry. We always come prepared. We carry this around in case we are not aware how long it has been since she ate. She will be up and at 'em in a few."

The server accepted the answer and walked away. Libby felt like she was in the dream and awake at the same time. The voices had gotten louder. She heard everything that was happening at the table, and could sense the actions of her mother, father, and the server.

"I'm glad that you knew bringing the inhaler was a good idea. Even though she stopped having those headaches when she was eleven, something compelled me to bring an inhaler with us, just in case."

It was quiet for a few moments.

"Shouldn't she be alert by now? It never took this long in the past. Maybe she's immune to the inhaler now. We haven't had to do this is so many years."

"Should we shake her?"

Libby just remained still and listened to her parents. The visions had stopped.

"Remember that whenever she suffered from one of her bad headaches, she would say that she saw visions of a fight between you and her aunt. She kept talking about and asking for some lady named Melanie. Then she finally stopped. No more bad dreams, and no more visons. I was glad that she did not equate those dreams with what really happened."

"That could have been disastrous. There's no telling what she might have wound up saying to teachers or her friends at school."

"It was good that we kept her home from school whenever it seemed like she was in really bad shape. And when she did go, I would pick her up often just so I could check out the vibe of the staff and students around her. Then I would take her to the ice cream shop to get a firsthand account of her day. Nothing ever seemed amiss. After a while it was obvious that she wasn't saying anything to anybody about her headaches."

"Why is she so still? Why didn't the inhaler work?"

"I don't know, but there might be trouble if she's not alert when the server comes back."

"He dropped off the dessert when he was last here, but he'll surely be back soon with the check. Maybe you should head him off. Just go to where he is and pay him there. Slip him a bunch of extra cash to keep him from coming back over here."

Her father left the table.

Libby felt a hand touch her shoulder. She knew that it was coming from across the table, and that her mother hadn't gotten up to sit next to her to try to soothingly or tenderly revive her. Libby was given two gentle shoves, but she forced herself to remain still and appear zoned out.

When her father returned, he asked "Any change?"

"No. She's still out of it. I've tried to wake her."

Her father sighed, and sounded a little panicked when he said, "My gosh. Maybe we shouldn't have done it. She was so young."

"We knew it was risky, but we had to have the procedure done. It was better for us to perform surgery on her to give her dissociative amnesia, than to take a bigger risk in having her know the truth. We had to do something to erase the traumatic experience that she encountered."

"Maybe we shouldn't talk about it here. What if she can hear us?"

"I don't think she can hear anything."

They stopped talking, and Libby could feel them looking at her, waiting for some indication that she was aware of their conversation.

They must have been satisfied that she was still out of it, because the exchange then continued.

"By the time that we finished the additional treatment course, she didn't even remember the incident. She kept having headaches, but then they finally stopped. We were home free at that point, and we had no worries. Then years later, who would expect that a genealogy project would come into play. That horrible project!"

"Yeah. Perfect timing on that! She was about to graduate. Everything with her and us was going according to plan. The inheritance could have gone on without a hitch. No obstacles. But look at where we are now. In Texas. Right next to Atheneum. A place that we knew that we had to avoid in order to—"

"Shhhh. Be quiet. I think she just moved. She might be coming to."

Her parents waited, but saw that they were wrong about her movements. She waited for them to reveal more, but they didn't say anything else.

After about three minutes, Libby started to make sporadic movements, wisely spacing them apart to make a slow appearance back into consciousness.

Chapter Fifteen
by Shontrell Wade

    After dinner, Libby had gone to her parents' hotel room after they insisted that they wanted to be sure that she was okay. They had told her that she had just fainted, and that she had only been out for about two minutes. She felt confident that they had believed that she had slowly became alert again, and that she had not been cognizant of their conversation. The three of them sat around making small talk. They talked about the weather, politics, current movies and television shows. It was ridiculous. Neither of them would break and admit that this was all a farce.

    Libby was sure that the invitation to their room was to see if she would slip up and repeat something that her parents said when they thought that she was out cold.

But Libby was no different. She only agreed to go there to see if they would let anything else slip out about what they had done to her in the past. It was not just about the procedure that they had done to remove certain aspects in her memory. It was also about what they had done to cause them to need her memory altered in the first place. Libby was there for one reason only — to hear what other lies her parents would tell her.

They'd talked into the wee hours of the night, without either of them dropping the façade. Libby had to admit to herself that they were all great at their performances. When it was clear that neither party was going to get what they had hoped for, Libby told her parents to rest well, and that she hoped to see them again at breakfast later that day.

However, Libby did not go back to her own hotel room. She had her purse with her when she went to dinner, and its contents were all that she needed right then. She had her house and car keys, her wallet, and cell phone. She had decided to just go back to her cottage. It was apparent that wherever she went, someone she knew was going to show up. Libby's thoughts told her that it was probably more convenient to just hide in plain sight. She would just go back to the hotel tomorrow to collect her stuff.

While she had been talking to her parents in their hotel room, her parents finally found a way to make it seem as though they wanted Libby to come back home with them, without actually saying it or actually asking her. Even though it wasn't an authentic offer, she still firmly refused. She had wanted them to ask her, because she wanted the appearance of having the upper hand. But moving back was not something that she had actually wanted to happen. Even when she had gone to Lacassine that past Wednesday, it was never in the hopes of that. She had just used Brandon's rude display from the night before to her advantage.

And he played right into Libby's hands. She knew that someone would track her movements there. At the time, she did not know who that someone would be, but she knew that the person would do something drastic after that. So while the kidnapping ordeal was fairly uncomfortable and slightly painful, it was a small price to pay for what she was really after. In Brandon's kidnapping scheme, he did his best to look like a tough guy, but his swift eschewal at Jane's house showed his true cowardice. He was going to have to do much better if he thought that he could outsmart Libby and get his hands on what they both wanted. But his retreat might be to give him time to come up with another plan to get rid of Libby and get the prize.

The townspeople of Atheneum could just keep thinking that she didn't belong, and that she was an outsider. But she was going to stay as long as she had to. Everyone would find out soon enough that she was not leaving until she got what was due to her.

Hearing from her parents that she was related to the Jades, made her slightly ill. Not because of the fact that the Jades were awful people, but because her parents were telling a blatant lie. Her mom was not the product of a Jade and a Sleuth. The liaison that took place and produced a mix of the families happened decades ago with Miriam Peck.

But Libby knew that her mother was not aware of how much dirt and deception that Libby had uncovered due to the genealogy project. So it made sense for her parents to lie, and do what they could to keep the truth from coming out.

Greystoke scratched on the screen outside of Libby's window, and mewled at her. She stretched and swung her legs off the bed and stood up. She bounded to the door and let him in. The cat wound through her legs and she reached down to pet him, scratching between his ears and listening to him purr.

Libby was ecstatic to see him again. She had been worried that maybe Brandon or Wilson had come by to do something to him, because she had not seen him that night that she had come home after her ordeal with them. "C'mon, big boy. Let's get you some breakfast."

After pouring kibble into Greystroke's bowl and fawning over him for a while, Libby showered, dressed, and left for a trek to Thirp's. The walk helped calm the thoughts skittering around her head and allowed her to think — namely about what her next moves should be, and how she needed to be on high alert at all times. Brandon had agreed to back off, but she knew not to trust him. Libby had the same sentiment with Jane. How had she ever trusted the woman and thought they could become friends? Even without knowing that she was the sister of two of her nemeses, Libby's gut was supposed to work better than that, and know that Jane was not someone in Atheneum that could have been her buddy.

Destroying the Jade family wouldn't be easy, and Libby knew not to even put those thoughts in her head. Atheneum may as well have been renamed Jadeville. Once George Sleuth left in 1948, the town was all theirs, and they have had sixty-seven years to keep it that way. With the bulk of the town in their pockets, they seemed invincible, and Libby didn't necessarily want them ruined entirely. She just wanted some of the wind knocked out of their sails.

She walked on, frowning in concentration. She didn't even remember entering the store, nor picking a k-pod flavor and putting it in the coffee machine. She was so caught up in her thoughts as she waited for it to brew, that she didn't realize anyone had come near where she was standing.

"Good morning, Miss Ferguson."

Libby whirled at the sound of the drawling bass. She was already off to a bad start of staying on high alert.

"Cah—" she said, catching herself before she got his formal name all the way out. "Good morning, Joshua," she recovered, and smiled at him.

If the rest of the town had shunned her, the policeman had kept her at arm's length. He'd never been rude to her, but he hadn't exactly been friendly to her. Now that she thought about it, he'd been ... watchful.

The bell over the front door chimed and they both looked in that direction. Brandon Jade had come in and went to the front counter to talk to Fred Thirp. Libby looked at Captain Smith and saw him scowl. Once he saw her looking at him his face went blank.

"Not a fan, huh?" Libby asked him.

He remained silent for a moment, appearing to choose his words wisely as he watched her. His face remained impassive and when he spoke, his tone was neutral. "Not exactly."

He shifted his weight to one leg and said, "It looks like it's going to rain any minute. Can I offer you a ride home?"

She blinked and looked outside. The sky was clear. "Uh, sure."

Brandon walked away from the counter before Libby walked over to pay for her coffee. Captain Smith led her outside, and they watched Brandon drive away before they walked and got into the officer's car.

She buckled her seatbelt and looked around the vehicle. "A Beetle. Not what I expected from a macho police captain."

"It's not much, but you don't have to ride in back," he said, making Libby laugh.

"It's my daughter's," he explained. "My car is in the shop. I'll get in my cruiser when I go on duty in a little while."

He backed out of the parking space. "How was your night? Still being treated like the new girl?" he asked, and Libby knew that the last part was his attempt at more humor. He knew that there was no way that things in Atheneum had changed for Libby since their conversation on the previous evening.

"I guess it's a little better," she said anyway. He nodded, and she looked out the window. "Just a little, though. This town is …" She searched for a word, but couldn't find one that adequately expressed her feelings. "It's something," she finally said.

"Yeah, that about sums it up," Captain Smith agreed.

"You didn't exactly roll out the welcome mat to me either, Captain," Libby said. "When I called in last year and said I thought someone had been in my house, the police force took its sweet time coming out, and you personally made me feel like a pariah when you did finally show up," adding a slight bit of harshness to let him know that she was still displeased with the state of affairs of that night.

He blew out a breath. "I'm sorry. And looking back, you do have every right to be mad." He pulled into her driveway and put the car in park. "I wasn't trying to give you a hard time. It had been a bad day. You aren't the only one the Jades give a hard time."

Libby raised an eyebrow. "You mean the police aren't employees of the Royal Family of Atheneum?"

He gave a wry smile. "You aren't the only *undesirable* around here."

She frowned. "Why would you be undesirable?"

He looked at her, seeming to scrutinize her before responding. "That's a conversation for another day."

"Okay, then." She wanted to pursue the issue, but sensed it would be futile. "Thank you for the ride, Captain, and saving me from this horrible rain."

Once she saw him look up at the sun and smile, she opened the car door and got out, shutting it behind her.

He rolled down the window, before she started to walk away. "Take care. And try to steer clear of the Jades."

Libby smirked before she turned and walked away. She had never mentioned to Captain Smith that she had any problems with the Jades, and yet he had just mentioned the family twice within mere minutes. The first time was especially suspect, because it didn't fit into what they were discussing. It seemed very convenient to Libby that the captain found an unwarranted way to bring the Jades into their conversation.

Most importantly, it let Libby know that she had better act fast and keep her eyes open in every direction.

***

Libby stood behind her desk, clenching her teeth and struggling to maintain her composure. "I am your boss now. Regardless of whether you like me or not, you will respect my position."

Wilson smirked. "You may be the boss for now, but for how long?" He moved closer, looking down at her. "You're still an outsider. A *nothing* in this town. Brandon agreed to back off, but I didn't."

"Get out," Libby said through pursed lips. Wilson walked to the door and paused with a hand on the knob. "I'll see you at the party tomorrow. Mrs. Grisham Patterson is punctual. Make sure you're there early to greet her. And dress appropriately. *Nothing green.*" He smiled at her and left, closing the door behind him.

Libby flopped into her chair and leaned back. *I really hate him*, she thought. Why hadn't she gone to the police about what they'd done to her and Poppy? He'd be out of her life. *No, he wouldn't*, she told herself. *Because the Jade money makes the rules in this town.*

The staff meeting had gone smoothly until the discussion turned to the release party for their most popular author. The manager of the venue had booked two events for the same night. The man had apologized profusely and even offered a substantial discount on her next event. Libby had been furious, but there was nothing to be done. Wilson had swept in to save the day, saying they could move the party to the Jade estate, the same one where the annual ball was held. In his gloating, it had come out that the event that bumped hers was being thrown by Brandon.

"A meeting of some investors and lawyers," Wilson said, waving a hand in the air. "A bunch of big words and legal jargon. We can have our party at my family's estate. It'll be a more intimate affair, one where we can appropriately fawn over our esteemed author."

He turned to Libby. "Don't you think that will be a much better venue for this type of event? I mean, the hall you chose is drab and so ... so ... utilitarian. Look at how much you spent on decorations to make it presentable."

He snapped his fingers. "Oh wait. This was your first time in charge of planning an event like this. That's okay. I'm sure you'll do better next time. I'll simply make a phone call when we're done here, and the *competent* staff will handle everything."

Half of the meeting attendees looked down at the table, seeming uncomfortable. The rest looked from Wilson to her, their faces wearing the same looks of shock.

Libby couldn't let Wilson get away with disrespecting her. That would set the wrong precedent for the rest of her staff.

"Wilson," she'd said, "I'd like to see you in my office after your phone call." She turned to the others. "Meeting adjourned." Without another word, she left the conference room.

Before she'd had time to take a deep breath and count to ten, Wilson had entered her office right behind her. He had apparently decided to skip his phone call. She had wanted to smack the smug look off his face when he said, "I'll be taking the rest of the day and tomorrow off to supervise preparations for the party."

With that, he turned and walked out of her office before she could say a word.

***

"Libby?"

Libby snapped out of her sleep and looked up and around from her desk chair. "Angela. Hi. What can I do for you?"

Angela closed the door and sat down in the chair across the desk from Libby. "I just wanted to see if you were okay. I heard about Wilson's antics in your meeting."

"I'll be fine when I calm down some more," Libby yawned and stretched her arms out. "I wouldn't be surprised if he and Brandon did this on purpose to make me look incompetent as the new deputy director under William Marquette."

Angela stood up. "I've got some things to do, so I'll let you go now. Tread lightly. You have already been a great boss, and you could go far in this industry once you get this management experience under your belt. HouBayou is a great company for you to do that at. But it won't happen if the Jades say otherwise. At least not in Atheneum. Or Texas, for that matter. They've got a lot of pull."

After Angela left, Libby made the necessary calls to let party invitees know about the last-minute change of venue. The party was still on. Once they were through it, she'd figure out what to do about the Jades.

Libby arrived home that evening to find Captain Smith waiting in her driveway. "What can I do for you, Captain?" she asked when she got out of her car.

"I understand there was a mix-up and your party got bumped to a different location."
She raised an eyebrow. "How did you hear about that?"

"Small town. People around here know you're going to sneeze before it comes out."

"That's the truth. What does the party have to do with the police?

"Nothing, really. Several of my officers have been hired to provide security on the grounds during your event."

"The Jades go all out, don't they? And I'm pretty sure Wilson is putting on this *lavish* affair to make me look bad." The policeman looked at her without saying anything, and once again, Libby felt like he was assessing her.

"Come on in and have a cup of coffee," she said, attempting to deflect his attention. "I'll warn you, though. All I have is instant. I prefer going out to get the good stuff."

He followed her inside and into the kitchen. She gestured for him to have a seat at the table while she filled a pot with water to put on the stove.

"The Jades are very influential," he said once she had prepared his mug of coffee and sat down across from him.

"I know," she said.

"They're one of the founding families."

"I know that too. One of four. The Jades are the last remaining in town."

He blew into the cup to cool the hot liquid. "You've been using your time in the library with Poppy to research town history."

She noted it was a statement and not a question. There weren't any secrets in Atheneum. Apparently, no one's business was his or her own. She shrugged. "I was curious. And it's interesting. One family remaining, allegedly having managed to get rid of two of the others after one sold out."

A look she couldn't read passed across his face, and then he asked her, "Why are you so interested in the town history?"

She hesitated. There was no way to tell him about her real connection to the town. And what if he was under the control of the Jades? "I'm a history buff," she said.

"Not going to admit to having ties to the town, are you?" Captain Smith asked her. "Think you can't trust me?"

Libby froze. "What do you mean?" she hedged. "What ties? And why shouldn't I trust you? You're the town's police captain."

"I know who you are," he glared at her. "I know who your family is. I understand your feelings about the Jades. I may be the only one in town who does."

Chapter Sixteen
by Patrick G Howard

Libby's alarm seemed to come particularly early today, even for five a.m. It sounded like annoying screeching, and she was sure that it was hated by everyone that heard that sound. The never-ending, Metallica concert loud honking, the garbage truck backup beeper, fingernails on the chalkboard, baby screaming on an airplane sound that just grates on raw nerves. It didn't matter what time of day it was, or what she was doing, all Libby needed was to hear that alarm sound on the television or radio, and her heart usually began pounding loudly in her chest and she wanted to throw a brick at something.

It didn't help that Libby spent the first part of the night tossing and turning, never really sleeping. And who could blame her? Her mind simply wouldn't shut off. On top of worrying about retaliation from Brandon or Wilson, and feeling like a sitting duck in her house, she kept on thinking about that conversation she had with the Captain yesterday. Then Libby became more curious than ever.

Eventually though, she finally fell into a sleep, but woke up to the incessant alarm noise feeling damp, hot, and confused. She touched her forehead and felt excessive moisture. Moving her hand across the top of her nightgown evidenced more wetness from sweat. It was practically drenched.

She was still breathing heavily as she raised her torso up a little and rested on her elbows. Libby blinked her eyes and looked around her bedroom as best she could in the dark. Nothing appeared to be moving, and she heard no sounds. She laid back down.

She realized that she had just had a bad dream, and that was why her nightgown was saturated. She wanted to make sense of what had happened in the dream, but there was no time to dwell on such a thing now. She had to get ready for what would surely be another dreadful day at work. She wondered who else hated being stuck in a job that they loathed. Living in a town where they didn't know who to trust? But Libby had no other choice at this time, and she had to get prepared to go.

As she began her morning grooming ritual, she was interrupted by her phone ringing. Annoyed, Libby wondered who would be calling at this time of the morning. As she looked at the Caller ID, a smile came over her face.

Libby answered, "Good morning, Captain."

Captain Smith replied, "Now, Libby. Didn't I ask you to call me Joshua?"

"My apologies. Good morning, Joshua," she said with a lilt in her voice and a glint in her eye.

He said, "That sounds so much nicer. I hope I didn't wake you."

They proceeded with obligatory small talk for a few minutes, bantering back and forth. Libby was enjoying the moments, and it seemed to her that Captain Smith was as well. She had momentarily forgotten about the nightmare she had. It didn't appear to her that he wanted to have a serious conversation. If a casual observer saw or heard any of this between them, they might say that the two of them were flirting.

Surely, not.

After a while, Captain Smith decided to get to the point of the call. He said, "Libby, I've been thinking about our conversation all night. I think it's time we laid all the cards on the table. No more secrets. No more beating around the bush. Could we talk over dinner tonight?"

Libby's heart was thumping in her chest again, but it was the good type; not like the heart pounding you experience from that dreadful alarm clock. Too many emotions were running through her mind and her body. She was excited and nervous at the same time, and couldn't really pinpoint and settle on one feeling. She didn't quite know what to say, but she knew she couldn't say no.

Libby replied with restrained excitement, and said, "That sounds nice."

Captain Smith said, "Great. I'll pick you up at 7:00."

"I'll see you then," she said, and hung up the phone.

Looking at the time, Libby realized that she had just spent thirty minutes talking on the phone with Captain Smith, and now she would surely be late for work. But she didn't really care. She didn't know what was so important that the captain wanted to discuss over dinner, but for the first time since she moved to Atheneum, it felt like she was going to get some answers. Maybe she would finally find a way to get what was due to her in this community.

But before that, there was a work day to get through. Ugh!

Libby arrived at work, and surprisingly, she made it on time. How that happened was anybody's guess, but some days you just have to be thankful for the victories that you are given. It wasn't in Libby's nature to complain, and she certainly wasn't going to start now.

Knowing that she had a busy day of reading and editing to do, and nervously anticipating an evening with Captain Smith, Libby began tapping away at her keyboard. Even though she made as much effort as she could, of course, she wasn't really paying much attention to her work. Her mind was a whirlwind of thoughts and she was merely going through the motions of her job; just doing her time until this evening. But regardless of how much she tried to concentrate on her work, she kept on coming back to one thought. Libby didn't believe in fate, destiny, or even karma for that matter, but she was certain about one thing — her life seemed to be taking a rather serendipitous turn.

And it was a really nice thought to have.

***

KNOCK! KNOCK! KNOCK! KNOCK! KNOCK!

Captain Smith had arrived, and Libby's heart felt like it was beating in her throat. She had been a ball of nerves all day trying to decide what to wear. Libby knew that it was only dinner and a conversation, but she wanted to look nice. But not too nice. She thought about how wearing the right thing, and fashion in general was always a conundrum for girls.

Libby had decided on, and was wearing a white dress with the lemon-yellow floral pattern. Simple and flirty, it was one her favorites. She accessorized her dress with a complementing malachite necklace and bracelet. Libby was one of those girls that didn't realize that she was pretty, no matter what she wore, but she would surely turn heads in this outfit.

Captain Smith must have agreed, as he complimented her on her choice as soon as she opened the door. He offered his arm and asked, "Are you ready?"

When they were in the car, Captain Smith asked if she would mind if they went some place a little out of the way. "After all, it would be best if we could have a nice, quiet, peaceful conversation, out of the way of prying eyes, and listening ears," he reasoned.

Although she was still unaware of what Captain Smith wanted to talk about, Libby agreed that would be best.

It was a nice country ride. They had been on the road quite a while, but Libby didn't seem to mind. She was enjoying the excursion. The twilight scenery was beautiful and the music on the radio put her in a relaxed mood. Libby couldn't remember the last time she felt this way.

After about half an hour of driving through the country, Libby could see neon lights in the distance. It was almost like a mirage in the desert. It reminded her a little bit of the Marfa ghost lights, and she wondered if that was their destination.

Just inside the city limits of Dime Box, Captain Smith pulled into the parking lot of The Lucky Duckling Chinese Restaurant. "I hope you like Chinese," he said.

Libby replied that she did. Not that it would have mattered to her, because they were there, and it was out of the way. Besides, Libby couldn't remember the last time she had eaten at a Chinese buffet, as there weren't too many great restaurants in Atheneum. It was the perfect choice for tonight. It looked like a casual and fun place, and she thought it would surely be delicious.

"Are you familiar with Dime Box at all?" Captain Smith asked Libby.

She smiled at him and said, "My only familiarity with Dime Box are the highway signs that we passed before the exit."

Captain Smith laughed and said, "Well I can say that it may not seem like the town would be known for its fine Chinese cuisine, but The Lucky Duckling is a very popular place. People drive from all over to sample their Far East fare. And no, I don't mean Far East Texas fare. While their entire menu is sure to please, they are most famous for their Sweet and Sour Chicken."

Libby licked her lips just from the thought, because she really did love chicken. She would eat chicken almost any way you could cook it — barbecued, broiled, baked, sautéed. She loved it on kabobs, in a creole, in a gumbo. You could pan fry it, deep fry it, or stir fry it. It could be pineapple chicken, lemon chicken, pepper chicken, chicken noodle soup, chicken stew, chicken salad, chicken and potatoes, or even a chicken sandwich. It didn't matter, as long as it was chicken. But when she ate Chinese, it was usually Sweet and Sour Chicken.

Libby wondered if Captain Smith knew that she loved chicken, and if that was why he chose this place.

The two of them made their way to a quiet booth in the back where they wouldn't be disturbed. They were greeted by their waiter, who offered a wine list. Since Libby didn't know much about wine, she asked Captain Smith to choose. He picked a nice bottle of Gewurztraminer. Libby was impressed by his choice — not because she had ever had this type of wine, but because it appeared so natural for him when he pronounced "Gewurztraminer."

And who would have thought to put a German wine with Chinese cuisine? *Certainly not me,* she thought.

While they were waiting for the bottle, Libby and Captain Smith decided to explore the buffet. Of course, Libby headed straight for the Sweet and Sour Chicken, while Captain Smith decided to start with a nice bowl of Egg Drop Soup.

As Captain Smith stood at the soup tureen, Libby finally fully noticed what a handsome man he was. She wasn't sure what kept her from seeing that before. He was a little over six feet tall, with dark hair, and a neatly trimmed moustache and goatee. Libby didn't usually go for facial hair, but it looked really nice on him. She also observed that he was always impeccably dressed when he was not in uniform. Wearing a starched shirt, and pleated slacks, Captain Smith always looked like a gentleman.

As Captain Smith was filling his bowl, Libby noticed that the duck sauce was near where he was standing. She went there and topped off her chicken with the delicious golden-orange nectar, and as she replaced the ladle, a rogue drop fell on the toe of Captain Smith's immaculately shined, size 11, cordovan colored, wing-tipped, left foot Florsheim shoe.

Her face must have been beet red, because she felt flushed and warm. She was embarrassed, but also slightly amused as Captain Smith looked down at the mess on his perfect shoe, and then up at her with one raised eyebrow, as if to say, "You did that on purpose, didn't you?"

They laughed, and even after the time they had already spent together in the last few days, it was certainly the ice-breaker they had been looking for.

Captain Smith and Libby returned to their table just as the waiter returned with their German wine. As Libby took the first sip, she was surprised at how delicious the Gewurztraminer was. It was fruity, sweet, and spicy all at once. It was the perfect choice for the delicious chicken dish she was about to enjoy.

They began to dine on their meals, all the while making small talk. Captain Smith was so easy to talk to, but Libby was self-conscious. She didn't want Captain Smith to think that she was a total flibbertigibbet, like many of the other girls he surely met daily in his line of work.

They kept the conversation safe at first. They talked about kitties, fire trucks, their wacky families, and other innocent, but interesting subjects. As well, Libby managed to avoid the subject that Captain Smith had brought them here to discuss, by bringing up her awful sleep from the night before.

"I had a very weird dream last night," Libby told Captain Smith. She told him about all of a sudden being the boss at HouBayou, even though Angela was there. "It was abnormal for Ms. Lamar to be a regular employee. She pretty much seemed to be me in the dream."

She went on to tell Captain Smith about the event with the famous author at the main Jade estate that Wilson was spearheading — although that event already happened last week at HouBayou.

"I woke up flustered and confused. Nothing made sense," she explained.

Captain Smith looked at her quizzically, and said, "It sounds normal to me — like a regular dream that most people have. We imagine things and see people there from our normal lives. And most of the time the situation in the dream doesn't make clear sense. But we wake up, get our bearings, and do not dwell too much on it."

"The weirdest part was that you were in the dream also," Libby said in a quick disregard to what Captain Smith had just stated. "You said something to me like, I know exactly who you are."

Libby was looking directly into Captain Smith's eyes. "I know that it was just a dream, but it felt, you know, kinda real. And for some reason it still does."

But just as Captain Smith started to either respond to this or bring the subject around to the important topic he had for her tonight, his phone rang. After looking at his display screen, he quickly stood up from the table. He looked down at Libby and said, "I'm sorry, but I have to take this. It's the mayor."

He walked to a quiet corner of the restaurant, but Libby was able to observe him throughout the entire time that he was on the phone. It was a rather lengthy conversation, but Libby thought, "How often do you get a call from the mayor?"

Captain Smith had a very serious look on his face as he hung up and walked back over to the table. He said, "We're going to have to finish our conversation some other time. The whole town of Atheneum is in chaos, and the police chief isn't answering his phone. I've got to go back and deal with the situation."

He pulled out his wallet and threw some bills on the table. He told Libby, "It's a long story, but it's a doozy. I'll tell you all about it on the drive back."

After Captain Smith explained the situation to him, the owner of the restaurant allowed him and Libby to take some food to-go. Captain Smith started the story once they were back on US-290, heading east.

"The situation in town actually started with the police chief," he said. "You see, he was relaxing after work, enjoying a few beverages with the buddies. He was across the creek at Sunny's. This is where cops like to go after their shift to wind down and tell stories to each other."

Captain Smith was already driving way past the posted speed limit, and Libby started feeling anxious. She grasped the long strap of her seat belt with her left hand.

"Well, the chief is known to be irresistibly charming, and is prone to a little jiggery-pokery in general," the captain continued. "As he was enjoying his time with the boys, someone that he had never seen before caught his wandering eye. He decided to go over and strike up a conversation. And knowing the chief like I do, I know that he felt like he was the best person to bring out the welcome wagon for this visitor or what-have-you. One thing led to another, and before long the chief called up his wife to tell her not to wait up for him, because he would be working late."

For the last part of the sentence, Captain Smith took both hands off the steering wheel to illustrate air quotes with his fingers. Libby's eyes widened as the car veered slightly toward a shoulder barricade. Despite what Captain Smith was doing with his hands, his eyes remained on the road, and he did not notice Libby's reaction. He kept on with the story.

"Of course, his wife knew what that meant. Upset that he was working late yet again, she called up her sister and asked her to come over to share a tub of ice cream with her. After she said that she would be over in a few minutes, her sister told her boyfriend of her plans, and that she would be back later.

"Well, her boyfriend now found himself lonely with nothing better to do, so he decided that he would go to Thirp's for some beverages and a couple of lottery tickets. He picked up two of his nephews on the way. When they arrived at the store, he told them to just hang out because he would only be a minute or two."

Captain Smith paused and shifted himself in his seat before resuming. "Now, we all know better than to leave the car running while you go into a store. And it's an especially bad idea to leave the car running with two teenage boys in the car. You might have guessed by now. The boys decided that they had plenty of time to take a joy ride, so joy riding they went. Of course, neither one of them had their driver's license yet, nor had either actually been behind the wheel before. What could go wrong, right?"

Captain Smith gave a short chuckle as he looked in the side mirror on his door. "Everything was going fine until the nephew that was driving decided to hit the gas to see what that car could do. That was a really big mistake. As you might imagine, when he accelerated, he lost control of the vehicle. The car started fishtailing and became uncontrollable. Swerving back and forth, he was momentarily able to straighten the path of the car. Straight into the path of an oncoming 18-wheeler, that is."

Libby looked at Captain Smith and forgot her own fear for the time. She wasn't thinking about his high speed for the moment.

"The boy cut the wheel just in time to miss the big truck, but unfortunately the car hit a curb. That caused him to lose control again. The car careened off the Dairy Queen sidewalk sign and headed straight for the bank time and temperature clock. You know the one — the one that always has the wrong temperature. The one that says it's 104 degrees in the middle of winter."

Libby knew exactly which bank and restaurant location that he was talking about.

"The car instead hit the pole that the bank sign was on, causing it to fall on the big transformer at the power transmission station next to it," Captain Smith exhaled. "This caused the transformer to explode, plunging the entire town of Atheneum into darkness, and the town into chaos."

Libby was enthralled by the story, but yet all that she could say to Captain Smith was "Wow."

The captain went on. "The police on duty couldn't seem to get control of the situation. They interviewed witnesses but kept getting all kinds of crazy reports. One of the employees at the Dairy Queen was no help. She said that she saw aliens landing at the supermarket. And the guy across the street from the bank said he saw a cattle stampede."

Libby laughed, and Captain Smith joined in. Once he gained his composure, he said, "Since the police couldn't get control of the situation, they tried to get ahold of the chief, but the chief wouldn't answer his phone. So, they called the mayor, and then the mayor called me."

His voice was quiet and serious as he said, "Sorry about dinner." He turned to look at Libby, but quickly faced the front windshield again.

Libby guessed it really didn't matter if they found the chief or not. He was probably in the wrong frame-of-mind to bring order to the chaos that was gripping Atheneum. The situation sounded pretty major to her. With her companion being the captain in a small-town police department, she accepted that it was up to him to go back and handle the situation.

***

Libby opened her eyes and saw that she was outside of her house, strapped to an ambulance gurney. Looking up at the two paramedics that were working on her, she heard one of them say, "We have a pulse now."

Libby couldn't remember anything. She recognized that she was in the front yard of her home, but she didn't know how she got there. Nor could she fathom what day it was. Libby was completely disoriented and confused. She thought, *"Oh, no! Is this another one of my dreams? This seems like the worst one yet."*

Just as she was about to be loaded into an ambulance, Captain Smith leaned over her with a concerned look on his face and asked, "Libby, are you all right?"

Dazed, she replied, "Do I know you?"

Chapter Seventeen
by Kristina DeShee Magelky

"It's me, Joshua. Captain Joshua Smith."

Libby blinked several times, struggling to connect the name with the kind face above her. As she stared, a sharp pain began throbbing right behind her eyes. There were black spots in her vision and everything started to blur. Her eyes felt heavier and heavier with each passing second. She suddenly felt very tired, wanting nothing more than to go to sleep. She tried to speak, but only a groan came out.

"Libby? Libby, are you okay? Libby!" the man said. She felt his hand on her arm, but reality was slowly slipping away.

"She's starting to seize," a second voice said. There was rustling and jostling around her along with the sound of machines beeping and footsteps on pavement. The second voice continued to talk, but the words were garbled and distant. In all honesty, Libby didn't care who was speaking as she slid ever closer to the darkness.

***

The roaring train didn't slow as it sped towards Libby. She looked around and found herself tied to the railroad tracks, like the old western cartoons she watched as a little girl. In it, the bank robber would always tie a beautiful woman, with her thick Southern accent and giant hoop skirt dress, to the tracks as the sheriff tried to stop the runaway train. However, Libby was far too panicked about the train heading toward her to inspect her clothes.

Closer and closer the train moved, jostling the tracks beneath Libby's back. She tried to focus her mind on wiggling her hands to free them, but her mind was too foggy. Her hands felt heavy and numb. She tried to scream for help, but her voice was hoarse. She knew her time was running out. She lay facing a curve on the track, allowing her to see the side of the approaching engine. Even through the terror and confusion, Libby saw the logo clear as day — Sleuth & Company. Below the block lettered words, the outlined drawing of an acorn sat surrounded by a dozen green, five-pointed stars. There was something familiar about the logo, but the rushing train forced her to try moving again.

A bright light flashed and Libby knew this was the end. She shut her eyes, hearing nothing but the blare of the horn. It was deafening, pushing out any other thoughts in her head. She braced for impact as the horn blasted one last time.

***

Libby's entire body jerked awake. Instantly, she knew she was in a hospital as soon as she saw two monitors situated next to the bed that she was laying in. She struggled to remember whether she was injured from the train hitting her, or from something else.

She took a minute to look around. Everything was white: the sheets, the walls, and the gown she wore. There were voices in the hallway and footsteps echoing outside the door, an indication that she probably was not imagining this place as the other side of death. Although she was confused, her body started to relax as she realized she might be safe.

"Welcome back," chimed a cheery voice. An older lady in scrubs, probably in her late fifties, came into Libby's line of focus. "Now, if you could try to stay in the land of the living for a little while longer, that would be great."

Libby tried to reply, but only a groan came out as the pain from a headache hit her with full force. Reaching for her head, she discovered her hands had been secured to the hospital bed. She pulled but to no avail.

Noticing her futile struggle, the nurse spoke again. "Just try to relax and stay calm. Do you know your name?"

"Libby," she rasped, as both her mouth and lips were dry.

"Do you know what day it is?"

The second question was more difficult. "Uh, I, um, I dunno ... argh, my head."

She tried to reach for her head again, but the restraints prevented her from moving more than a couple of inches. The nurse moved to the side of the bed to release one of Libby's wrists.

"Your head is a body part, not a date," the nurse joked lightly.

Under different circumstances, Libby would have actually laughed. However, only a pained groan came out as the nurse said, "I understood what you meant. The headache is probably from the accident or the medication. Let me give you something for the pain."

Libby watched as the nurse grabbed a bottle containing some type of clear solution from a rolling cart that was in the room. She stuck a needle into the bottle and then placed the needle into Libby's IV. She watched the nurse as she started to remove the restraints from Libby's other wrist and both her feet.

She was surprised at how quickly the pain started to subside, clearing up the fog in her mind. Libby asked, "What happened?"

"The paramedics said you were found unconscious in front of your house and started to seize while they were transferring you to the ambulance," the nurse explained. "They gave you a few milligrams of Lorazepam to stop it, but then you went into cardiac arrest. You were revived in less than a minute, but you have been in and out of consciousness for the last hour or so."

Libby tried to sit up, but the nurse pushed her back gently. "The doctor will be in here shortly to answer any more questions, but your body needs to rest. Please?"

"Okay," Libby agreed, far too exhausted to argue with the woman.

"Excellent," the nurse said, picking up a stack of paperwork. "I'll be back by in a few minutes for some vitals." She swept out of the room with her cart, leaving Libby to her thoughts.

Trying to backtrack, Libby began to recall details of the evening. She'd been on a date with Captain Smith; that much was certain. He'd dropped her off at her house, walking her part way up the walkway. They'd shared a chaste kiss before he left quickly to go take care of the chaos in town. It was then that everything got hazy.

Libby remembered it was dark going up the walkway, likely from the events from earlier in the evening, but the lights from the neighboring towns kept it from being pitch black. Then, she remembered what she thought was a black snake on the ground. It wasn't moving. She remembered feeling concerned because the darkness hid the snake's pattern as well as its head, but she also felt confused because this snake was far thicker than any she'd encountered around her house before. The largest snake she'd seen in the garden was a garter snake, and even that was not very thick.

Then she remembered thinking that it must not be a snake but a hose. Or a tube. Or something inanimate. However, her speculations were interrupted by lights flicking on around her. She started to look up, but her body was suddenly shoved forward and hit the ground. There was searing pain, her leg muscles cramped, and then everything was dark again.

She had been shoved. Hard! She didn't just trip on a hose, or whatever that was, she was attacked! And she was sure that whoever shoved her, the Jades were surely behind it. The problem was that there were too many holes in her memory, no proof, and no one who would back her up. What was she going to do? Was she going to be looking over her shoulder for the rest of her time in Atheneum?

Libby's thoughts were interrupted by the door opening. A completely bald man with dark skin, and a crisp white jacket over his maroon scrubs walked in and picked up the clipboard at the end of her bed.

"Good day, I'm Dr. Sage. And you are ... Ferguson. Libby Ferguson," he read off. Libby nodded, so he continued talking. "Well, it looks like you had quite the night. Report says you had a downed power line in your yard. Electrocution, seizure, cardiac arrest — honestly, I'm surprised you are still coherent."

"I was electrocuted?" she croaked.

"Yes," he said, not looking up from the paperwork. "There is a burn on your arm, likely from where the electricity entered you. According to your boyfriend, he found you inches away, so we believe you must have tripped and landed close enough to be in the path—"

"My boyfriend?" Libby interrupted dumbly.

Dr. Sage finally looked up frowning. "Captain Smith was the first on the scene. He said he dropped you off after a date you two went on, but you left your doggie bag in his car. He said he turned around at the end of your street and headed back to your home to give it to you. When he found you, he called the paramedics and then escorted them here. He stayed as long as he could, but apparently, he still had a call he needed to tend to."

"Oh, right," Libby said, remembering the issue with the police chief that caused the premature ending of said date. Although she was still processing the thought of Captain Smith being identified as her boyfriend, she was more curious about her health. "So, I'm okay now? Or, I'm going to be okay?"

"We'd like to keep you here at least two more nights for observation," the doctor reported. "As the nurse said, you went into cardiac arrest after a dose of lorazepam, which we believe was a severe allergic reaction. However, the seizure was likely just a delayed effect from being electrocuted by over two hundred volts. If we don't see another seizure and your test results come back confirming our suspicions of an allergic reaction and not a seizure disorder, you'll be free to leave after that."

Libby nodded as the doctor put the paperwork down and checked her over. He listened to her heart, checked her eyes, and removed the bandage from her left forearm to inspect the wound. The skin was raw underneath and stung as the air hit it. Dr. Sage explained the electrical shock left a superficial second-degree burn, causing the pain and blistering, but would have very little scarring. He supposed it was because there was no prolonged exposure to the current.

As he finished up and advised her to rest some more, Libby immediately got to thinking — where did the power line come from? The lines were near the street and she remembered they were quite thick. If a power line broke, it should have landed closer to the street, not thirty feet up the walkway.

Unless someone moved it, she thought to herself. *No, unless one of the Jades moved it*, she corrected herself. She didn't trip — she was pushed. How else could she explain the force she felt from behind that made her fall as she turned to look at the power being restored around her?

Libby felt her stomach knot up. She had been lucky. She probably would have been dead if Captain Smith hadn't come back with her food. She was even luckier that he was a police officer with a direct line to emergency services. The Jades were close to getting what they wanted yet again — but they failed. They were determined, and she knew they'd stop at nothing. Once they discovered that she had survived, Libby knew they would try twice as hard to get rid of her. That thought chilled her. They had no qualms about kidnapping her, and now she knew they had none about murder either. Living here was getting too dangerous.

A fiery anger started to bubble up inside of her. She could run from the Jades, but then she was giving them exactly what they wanted. Atheneum was as much her home as it was theirs and they had no right to say otherwise. She wasn't going to let them win without a fight.

Feeling more determined than ever to shed some light on the ugly truth behind the Jades, Libby fell into an uneasy sleep, although she did not dream that night. She was able to escape reality for a few hours.

***

Hospitals had always reminded Libby of her parents and the profession she'd refused, so it went without saying that Libby was ready to leave the hospital as soon as possible.

She was checked over by Dr. Sage once again and was given a clean bill of health. Although he was confident the seizure and heart failure were isolated incidents, he advised her to watch for early signs of any additional incidences or cardiac distress. Since Libby was young and healthy, there was no reason to believe they would affect her health long term.

As Dr. Sage gave with his final thoughts, a knock echoed through the room. After asking the person to come in, Libby was surprised but thrilled to see Captain Smith's face appear in the doorway.

"Hey," he smiled.

"Hey," she blushed back. Dr. Sage chuckled at the shy pair before saying something about needing to get the nurse to bring the discharge papers and making a quick exit.

Breaking the awkward silence, Libby blurted out, "What are you doing here?"

"I heard you would probably be discharged today, so I came to offer you a ride home," Captain Smith said.

"I suppose that would be fine. After all, the last time you drove me home, you ended up saving my life," Libby joked.

Captain Smith smiled gravely. "Yes. You really had me scared. I thought you were gone."

"It's gonna take more than a little electricity to get rid of me," Libby muttered, but heard the deep emotion behind the banter.

"Let's hope nothing else does. I kind of like having you around," Captain Smith said quietly.

Libby couldn't help but smile. "Well, I kind of like being around here."

"Even with the Jades trying to run you out of town?" he asked.

Even with the Jades trying to kill me, she thought. Instead she chuckled and said, "They'll just have to get used to me staying here."

"Good," he agreed. It was then that Captain Smith seemed to notice the hospital gown Libby was wearing, because he averted his eyes. "Why don't I wait in the hallway while you get dressed?"

Libby nodded and Captain Smith took his exit. She'd just finished pulling her shoes on when the nurse knocked on the door with the discharge papers. A few signatures and several papers with information about possible side effects to look for, and Libby was finally being escorted out of the room in a wheelchair pushed by Captain Smith.

They made their way downstairs, chatting about his night. With the power back on, he dealt with the incident at the Dairy Queen and bank, a few burglaries that had taken place, and one accident on Main Street from the street lights that were out before he finally went searching for the police chief.

He decided to check Sunny's first, for the off-chance that the chief had returned there. Of course he knew right where to go to find him, but not before his angry wife had already arrived. Captain Smith laughed as he described finding the large man cowering in the corner of Sunny's place while his tiny sprite of a wife yelled at him. From what she had been spewing, she refused to believe that his phone had died while he was working late, and without any power anywhere, he could not charge it. He claimed that he had only been out checking on residents and looking out for their well-being during the blackout.

Libby listened to Captain Smith's story with joy. After what happened two nights ago, it felt good to have something as normal as being regaled by the adventures of a police officer's night while being wheeled down a hallway.

They had almost made it to the front doors when a large painting in the foyer caught Libby's eye. It covered the entire wall opposite the entrance so everyone entering the building would see it just below the hospital name and logo. Libby asked Captain Smith to take her to examine it.

The painting was of a woman who looked to be in her thirties, with raven hair pulled back in a fancy coif, seated in a chair with her hands placed delicately on her lap. She was dressed in an emerald gown, with puffed shoulders atop tight sleeves, and a high, buttoned-up neck that made Libby guess that the portrait was set in the early 1900s. The table beside the woman held a stack of books with medical titles etched in each.

"Lilly Peck, the founder of the hospital," Captain Smith answered Libby's unspoken question. "Back when the town was founded, the doctor was happy to make house calls. However, as the town grew, Lilly used her influence to raise money to build the first hospital. It was quite a feat in those days and even with all the tragedy in her life, she was still such a generous person. It was because of her that my grandparents named my mom Lilly. They always used to say, 'Never was there a Sleuth sweeter than Lilly; altruistic was her middle name.'"

"Lilly Peck? The same Lilly Peck who disappeared while swimming?" Libby asked.

"The very same," he nodded. "I know you know the circumstances around her disappearance were questionable with all the feuding over land around here, but the only reason the Jades haven't demanded the picture be removed is because her last name isn't Sleuth. Besides the town would have a conniption fit if it was removed."

He turned to look at the entrance and said, "I'll pull the car up so you don't have to walk." But once he turned again and looked down at her, his voice changed to slightly panicked as he said, "You're looking a little tired. Are you alright?" He reached his hand out and cupped her jaw.

Libby realized she'd been holding her breath as she had listened to him talk about Lilly Peck. Her face felt hot under his cool palm and she was sure she was redder than a watermelon at the peak of summer.

"Yes, I'm fine," Libby tried to smile brightly and brush it off. "You get the car and I'll just wait for you here. Really, Joshua. I'm fine."

Captain Smith nodded, but she could tell he didn't believe her completely. She expected him to question her more, but he didn't. Instead, he turned and exited the building without another word, leaving Libby to sit in front of the picture for a few more minutes.

Now that she knew who was in the portrait, she realized that it probably had been taken in the late 1930s or early 1940s. The story of Lilly's death was certainly fascinating and tragic, but not new. The book Poppy wrote explained the events in a distinct light. However, seeing the silver bracelet with the star, acorn, and key painted on the wrist of Lilly Peck was certainly a surprise Libby was not expecting.

Chapter Eighteen
by Dean Larson

It felt good to be sitting in her own kitchen sipping tea, Greystoke curled around her ankles. Until now, Libby had never truly appreciated her kitchen as a quiet sanctuary where she could think her thoughts uninterrupted by the demands of others. She had been so busy trying to get people to accept her, to like to her, she wasn't even aware that she had created a place where she belonged, right here in her kitchen.

With her cat, of course. The thought warmed her, and she reached down to scratch Greystoke behind the ears.

The events of the last two days had been spinning around in her head, and she was trying to relax and sort them out. Foremost in her thoughts, of course, was her having been electrocuted and almost dying. Had someone set things up to get rid of her, making it look like an accident? Last night, as she lay in bed in the hospital, she was so sure that she had been pushed, but now, in the light of day, her certainty was starting to waver.

She was nibbling on a grasshopper cookie, lost in thought, when her phone rang. "Good afternoon, this is Libby," she said without looking at the Caller ID.

"Hi Libby. It's Joshua," Captain Smith said, and Libby rolled her eyes. "I was wondering if I could talk with you this afternoon. I'd like to see you for several reasons, not the least of which is to reassure myself that you're okay. There are some other things I'd like to discuss as well. We didn't have a lot of time at the hospital or at your house this morning."

"Of course you can talk to me," Libby informed him, trying not to sound perturbed. "Are you going to come back over here? You know you are always welcome," she lied, and followed it up with another one. "Or at least I hope you know that."

"Actually, I'm already on my way," he said in a voice warmer than before. "I was hoping you'd be there, but I didn't want to simply show up and knock at the door. I'll see you in about ten minutes."

"Okay then. Bye," she said, hanging up. Annoyed, Libby brushed the crumbs off the green and white checkered tablecloth and got up to refill and turn the teapot back on. She then did a run-through of the short hallway and living room. She got done straightening as he knocked on the door. After a prolonged and fake "I'm so glad you are here" hug, Libby led Captain Smith to the kitchen, and offered him some cookies along with the tea.

Across the table from one another, simply staring into each other's eyes for a time, they simultaneously picked up their respective cups. The unplanned gesture broke the spell and sent them into peals of laughter, letting go of some of the tension that Libby felt.

"I was actually going to call you, Joshua," Libby said, "because I wanted to talk to you as well. Particularly about the incident out front two nights ago. The hospital staff called it an accident, but my memories of what happened are vague and I don't know whether accident is the right term. My thoughts are all over the place. Do you think it was accidental that I fell on the cable?"

Libby really had planned to call Captain Smith to talk about the incident, because she wanted to know his thoughts, or see what he could do for her. But she wanted all conversation about it to occur over the phone. She was not really comfortable with him being at her house again. She was apprehensive about the items she had hidden there, but more so about the ominous dream that she had three nights prior. Just as she told him at the restaurant, the nightmare felt so real, and it was as though his words were genuine — *I know exactly who you are.*

"To tell you the truth, that's why I came over," Captain Smith replied, bringing Libby back to attention. "Something wasn't right about what happened, and I'd like to explore events more closely. Start at the beginning, and we'll walk through the events one at a time. I'll interrupt if I don't understand something."

She cleared her throat and began, "Just after you left to attend to the disturbance downtown, I walked up the sidewalk. I remember that it was really dark, the only gleam was from the reflection of the moonlight. In the dimness, I saw the cable and my first thought was that it was a snake. That didn't make any sense, so I stopped and looked at it for a moment. It didn't move. I looked more closely and thought it was a black hose or some such, which didn't seem right because I don't own a black hose."

Captain Smith nodded, encouraging her to continue, his eyes intent as if pulling the story from her.

"I bent over the hose ... well, wire as it turned out ... to see what it was, and here is where things get fuzzy." Libby closed her eyes, as though she was trying to better visualize and remember the details of the incident. "As I bent, I either tripped and fell on the wire, or ..."

"Yes. Go on."

"Either I tripped, or I was pushed down on the wire," Libby said after she opened her eyes. "And Joshua, what I really think is that someone pushed me so that I'd be electrocuted!" She took a half-sobbing breath and went on, "And I *did* get electrocuted! I nearly died!"

Libby forced herself to hold in the tears that were attempting to come out. She was determined not to show any weakness. With the upcoming plans that she had, she was not going to let Captain Smith see her in that kind of state. She cleared her throat and hoped that her voice would not be shaky. "Last night, as I lay in bed, I was absolutely sure that I had been pushed, but today, with the sun shining, I'm not so sure. Can you help me find out what happened? Please?"

"Let's go out and have a look," Captain Smith said, in a somewhat paternal, protective voice.

Once outside, they stood on the front steps, surveying the scene before them. From an investigative standpoint, it was not a welcome sight. The wire in question had been removed by the power company, who left behind tire tracks, footprints, and nothing of the possible crime scene as it was the night before. Added to that were the signs that the ambulance attendants had been there and, of course, even Captain Smith's footprints seemed to run in all directions. It was just a mess.

Descending the steps, Captain Smith told Libby to stay on the porch and as he started walking the perimeter, his gaze was not just on the ground, but also went up the power poles, back down to the bushes, as well as the ground. He spent a long time examining the power pole, top to bottom. Libby stood quietly, arms folded in front of herself, but intently watching him as he moved about the yard, resembling a hunter stalking his prey. That thought made her shiver as she recalled that she might very well be someone's prey. At last, he returned to the steps.

"What did you find?" Libby asked.

"Pretty much what you'd expect. I wish I'd paid better attention that night, but with you there, lying on the ground, nothing else registered. The utility crew stampeded over anything that might have indicated the presence of an assailant, so the next thing I'll need to do is interview the crew that was here and have them help me recreate the scene and answer some questions," said Captain Smith, still looking intently at the yard. "It's not long until the night-shift utility crews start coming in, so I should be able to find them all together. I can talk to them while I'm still on duty until eleven."

Turning to Libby, he said, "I'm sorry I need to leave. I really enjoyed the little time we had sipping our tea, but I'll have to get right after this while it's still fresh in everyone's mind. I'll call as soon as I get something, one way or the other." He gave her a hug and, with a sigh, headed for the squad car. After he backed out into the street, he stopped for a moment to stare at the power pole again, then drove off.

Libby waved and started to turn back into the house. But something across the street had caught her eye. She was sure that she could see someone hiding in the bushes on the sidewalk in front of the house. They must have noticed her looking, because the person remained stock-still. After waiting and staring at the bush for about two minutes with no movement, it made Libby think that perhaps it was not the silhouette of a person that she was seeing, and maybe her eyes were playing tricks on her.

She went into her house, and immediately went to the living room window, which overlooked the front yard. The blinds were already open, so she picked a place where she could discreetly look out without the person being able to see her watching. By the time she got there, that area of the bushes was already different, and the person was gone. They must have taken their opportunity to get out while her back was turned, and she was walking in the house.

Libby ran back out of the front door and looked both ways down the street. She did not see any people at all. How had the person been so swift in their getaway?

She went back inside, sat on the couch with her cat, and began thinking about her situation. *Somebody is definitely trying to drive me out of Atheneum, that much is clear, and they're willing to go to any lengths to make it happen*, she mused. She sat, quietly petting Greystoke at her side and reliving the time since her life took such a dramatic turn.

***

That fateful Fall semester of 2012, the genealogy project assignment in one of her history classes seemed like it would be interesting and enjoyable. However, when the data came back and Libby found out more than she had bargained for, the pain and confusion were almost unbearable. Her mother had never been particularly warm toward her, and she thought that she would finally have an explanation for it.

Until the report came back.

She cried for days, her world turned on its head. After a while, though, tears of abandonment turned into a burning anger at having been betrayed as she mentally replayed all the times that her mother had been distant or cruel or indifferent, never understanding what she had done to be treated in that way.

While at home for Thanksgiving break that tragic semester, Libby became more and more angry at her mother until, unable to contain her feelings any longer, she decided to confront her. She padded around the huge house looking for her. Finally, she flung the front door open and looked out, only to find the cars all gone. She checked the garage and got the same result. She slammed the door closed, and turning on her heel, she began marching around the house, room to room, shouting her rage, until she came to her parents' bedroom. She walked in and stopped in her tracks. If she could find her birth certificate, maybe she could get some answers. Her parents had not wanted to tell her anything when she first got there that week and told them that she needed to know some family names and such for her project. She decided that this was the perfect opportunity to find out things on her own.

She spun, ran to the stairs and down to her parents' office where she started carefully, but deliberately began going through both of their desks.

Nothing!

In frustration, she looked around the room until her eyes landed on the painting of zinnias in a vase hanging on the wall by the window.

The safe!

Yes! The picture hid the safe.

Years ago, she had learned the combination to the safe and it became a game to sneak into the office and open it. However, once it became easy to enter, the game got to be a bore so she stopped playing it. There was nothing in the safe that interested her, only the challenge of opening it. She hadn't so much as peeked at it since she was twelve years old. If her parents hadn't changed the combination, she could check it and see if the answers to her questions might be found inside.

She removed the picture. With her heart in her throat, she spun the dial, stopping at the numbers as she remembered them. There was a distinct click, so she tried the handle. It turned, and the door swung open. With a blend of self-satisfaction at having opened the safe, and butterflies of apprehension in her stomach at what she might find, she began to remove the contents and place them on the desk. Among the other items, like the good jewelry, there was a brown accordion folder with an elastic binder around it. The word "Sleuth" was written on the outside in smudged, and barely legible pencil.

She placed the folder on the desk, removed the binder, and started to carefully examine the papers inside. Right at the top, she found a copy of the Sleuth will, describing the conditions of inheritance of the Sleuth land. She read the whole document; every detail. When she got to the back page and found the name of the person that was the sole heir to the Sleuth fortune, she recoiled in shock and wonder. *"Why are my parents pretending that they know nothing of their lineage? Why is it both of them pretending not to have family? Even if my mother wanted to hide this inheritance from me and Richie, what is the reason that my father claims no relatives? One doesn't seem to have anything to do with the other. Why is this being held secret?"*

Putting the will to the side and digging deeper into the folder, she found several more copies of the will. The original document contained the conditions of inheritance as well as what was bequeathed to the heir. A single heir.

She was stunned! She couldn't think, or even feel, and sat staring into space. The implications of what little she already found out in the genealogy project, put together with what was in the will, told her the ugly truth of what was happening.

She went back to the folder to see what else she could find. Beneath the copies of the will, there were some old newspaper clippings with the headlines: *"Local Woman and Daughter Disappear."*

She read on, *"Amelia Schickle, a resident of Atheneum, TX, and her four-year-old daughter Penny were aboard a train headed for Baton Rouge,*

LA, on their way to see a friend, when they disappeared. The friend, Lorelei Ferguson, waited for them at the depot stop in Lake Charles, LA, but they never appeared. Calls made to other train stops on the way to Baton Rouge did not reveal the pair. The police were alerted by Mrs. Ferguson and a search was begun."

The other articles were much the same, but the last had added the statement, *"If Mrs. Shickle is not found, the case will be turned over to Missing Persons for further investigation."*

Libby's mind went wild with the new information. She pulled out her cell phone and carefully took pictures of the documents, articles, and notes her mother had written, took what she needed, then placed the rest back in the safe.

While in the presence of her parents and her brother, Libby kept a pleasant demeanor for the rest of the school break. However, she snuck around the house secretly gathering items to use for DNA testing once she was back at the university. It was hard to concentrate on her other classes and prepare for her upcoming finals. She remained in a state of anxiety — *until the report came back.*

***

With a deep sigh, she settled back some more into the couch, and Greystoke hopped up into her lap. She sat, biting her lower lip, stroking the purring cat, lost in thought.

When she first came to Atheneum and found people so unwelcoming, she felt lost and afraid. "*Maybe I was extra sensitive due to the information that I had just found out about myself — and my mother. On top of that, I wound up in the very town that had a tremendous bearing on my life, and my future,*" she thought, nodding her head, "*and to this very day, I still do not know how that happened.*"

As she contemplated further, however, she became angry at one gnawing aspect; "*Even with the shunning of other townspeople and coworkers, the treatment I received at the hands of the Jades was something else completely! That was no suppressed emotion! The Jade apes purposefully tried to hurt and intimidate me to ... to what?*" she mused. "*Leave Atheneum? Why? I have thought and thought about the situation numerous times, but I still cannot figure it out. I do not know how anything would benefit them if I was not here!*

"*I'm helpless because I don't have enough information about who is responsible for what. I need to look at all the people who were involved in my life in a new light. Who is it that would stand to gain if I am gone? One thing is for sure, it wouldn't be me, and I do not plan to let that happen!*" Libby continued her thoughts with a rage that was starting to seethe through her.

In the middle of her ponderance, her cell phone rang. It was Captain Smith. "Libby, I need to talk with you. Now. Can I come over again?" He sounded very serious.

"Do you have news?" asked Libby, trying to mask the rage and tightness forming in her stomach.

"Not that I'd care to talk about on the phone. I'll be there in less than half an hour," he said, hanging up without actually receiving permission to come back to Libby's house.

About twenty minutes later, Captain Smith rolled up in his squad car. Libby, watching from the door and trying to keep the butterflies at bay, stepped out on the porch and waited for him to make his way to her. She held the door open for him, and they both went into the kitchen.

"I was able to interview several of the utility workers about what they found here," Captain Smith got right to the point. "They said they that it odd was that the wire would have come to rest where it did — right in that walking path. It should have dropped straight down, out by the curb. I asked them why the wire came down at all! The disturbances weren't even here by your house!"

Although it did not seem that he was doing it on purpose, Captain Smith must have realized that his voice was getting elevated. He palmed his temples with his left hand, rubbed his eyes, and then slowly slid his hand down to his chin before calmly saying, "None of them had an answer for that. They weren't looking for clues, so they didn't really see anything of importance, I guess. But the moving of the wire was more than enough information."

He looked Libby straight in the eyes, piercingly, and said: "Libby, someone tried to get rid of you. And in a way that would look like an accident."

Libby felt the blood drain from her face as reality sunk in. This was no longer a "suppose someone was trying to harm me" scenario — it was the real thing. She leaned over and put her head into her hands as her elbows rested on the kitchen island. She felt weak, afraid, and filled with rage all at the same time. Captain Smith simply watched her.

Finally, she said, "I thought so. I knew I had been pushed but didn't want to believe it." She had not moved her hands away from her head, nor stood straight up.

Captain Smith didn't respond, just still watched her. He eventually asked, "Libby, do you know of any reason that someone would be trying to hurt you in this way?"

"No! Why would someone want to do that? I've never done anything but move here," she said, raising up and turning around to face Captain Smith before continuing. "Although from the reaction of the locals, especially the Jades, that seems to have been a good enough reason. I haven't got any idea why anyone would want to take it so far!"

Captain Smith sat back in his chair, considering. "Well, that certainly doesn't help us with a motive. Perhaps if we can find out 'who', we'll come up with the 'why.'"

He paused and put his hands on the back of his neck and intertwined his fingers. "You mention the Jades, but what exactly would be their goal in harming you? I am not particularly fond of some members of that family, but there seems to be some heavy animosity between them and you. Why is that? It has to be more significant than harassing the new girl in town. Is there any background that you can provide to say why you think that they would want to hurt you?

Libby realized that Captain Smith was not aware of the kidnapping and brutal treatment that they gave her, and she knew that there was still no reason to tell him.

She tried instead to change the direction of the conversation. "I have a question," she said. "What happened to Bonnie? There was no body recovered at the scene of the train wreck, I understand. Were the Jades or someone trying to do to her the same sort of thing that's been happening to me?" she asked, quickly ruing the fact that she again mentioned her nemesis family when she was supposed to be steering the conversation away from them.

"We don't know," Captain Smith answered. "For right now, it's being called a property crime since there was no body and there were no witnesses. I thought we'd find her inside the car, but there was nothing. It's still an ongoing investigation."

Captain Smith sat forward in his chair and looked straight at Libby with his eyebrows furrowed. "Why would you think that the Jades harmed her?" he asked. "She is a Jade," he said before clearing his throat and relaxing his face again. "But I guess perhaps you wouldn't necessarily know that."

Libby did remember that it was mentioned by Poppy to Brandon during the kidnapping ordeal, but she never got a chance to find out the familial connection.

"At any rate, I could spend a little time with your two favorite Jade boys if you think I need to," Captain Smith said. "I can put a little heat on them to see if we can get a break on your incident, and on Bonnie's as well. If anything, they can at least tell me if they've heard anything around town about these two incidents. Is there anyone else we should look into?"

"My cousin, Jacob," Libby said without hesitation. "He was my keeper while I was in college, after basically following me there." She got a faraway look in her eyes before she spoke again. "Towards the end, he kind of seemed like more of a spy than anything else," she said.

She ruminated some more. "When we were kids, he lived with us occasionally because his mother both worked and went to school and was not home enough to take care of him. He was an extremely angry boy and he took great delight in bullying my brother and me. When we got older the bullying stopped, and I wanted to have as little contact with him as possible. But then there he was — enrolling in the same college as me."

After more quiet thinking she said, "Since I moved here and Jacob showed up, something happened to him. I don't know what, but he changed. It was almost as if he had switched sides. I found him talking to Poppy once, and also saw him in a car with Brandon and Wilson.

"Did he switch sides?" Libby asked quietly and seemed to be questioning herself. "I don't know. I guess he ... really could ..."

"Alright, Libby," Captain Smith interrupted her verbal reverie. "I've got plenty to get started on. While we're turning over rocks, looking for information, please be careful. Lock your doors, don't go for any long walks in isolated places, that sort of thing. I know you work with Wilson, but please use discretion. You'll gain nothing by being an even bigger target than you already are."

He rose, as did Libby, and he held her in his arms for a time, then, without saying anything, he left. Libby stood staring after him and thought, *"Now we'll get things rolling and some people will get what they deserve. Including me. He'll help me, even if he doesn't know he's doing it."*

She turned and sat on the couch, taking Greystoke into her lap, a satisfied smile on her face.

Chapter Nineteen
by Ramal Anglin

Libby discreetly lifted a slat of the blinds in one of her living room windows. Again she saw the same thing as she had in the last three hours. There was an Atheneum Police Department patrol car backed up into her driveway. Car number 1030 — Captain Smith's car.

Libby had spoken with Captain Smith one more time after he left her house that second time. She called him on the phone and asked him about the possibility of having a police officer stay with her throughout the night. He said that he could have officers drive on her street throughout their shift and check on her that way.

"But bad things could happen very quickly, and someone could come attack me while the officers are in-between rides," Libby bemoaned.

"You know yourself how bad the Jades are, and I am fearful of staying here alone."

He told her that unfortunately, regular patrols were the best that he could do. "The department just does not have the manpower to have officers staying in one set location for the night. I need all of the staffed personnel serving the whole town — not just one person. I'm sorry."

Libby used her fakest, saddest voice to tell him that she understood. She hung up with him and made herself a small dinner. After eating, she got herself ready for bed, so that she could turn off all of the lights. She wanted the house as dark and quiet as possible, so that she could stay close to a window and be aware of movements outside and hear any noises out there as well.

But before long, Captain Smith had come to her house himself, sitting guard in her driveway. She had first saw his car right before midnight. Now at almost 3 a.m., he was still here. She smirked each time that she peeked out and saw him. She thought, *putty in my hands*, since he apparently decided to volunteer his own time once his shift ended. From her view, she could see his silhouette in the dark, without him being aware that she was watching. So far, each time that she looked, he was moving around enough for her to know that he was fully awake, and did not fall asleep during the watch.

At the same time, she was a little peeved that she had not seen or heard him walk around the house to check for any signs of discord. *Shouldn't that be in his first instinct to do so?*

When he had arrived, he did not knock on the door to inform her that he was going to sit watch in her driveway for the night. She knew that he had no way of knowing if she was asleep or not, and surely did not want to disturb her. Maybe he also thought that she would be frightened if she heard someone skulking about the house, after she had called to ask for protection during that night. It was plausible, but she was still finding it hard to give him the benefit of the doubt.

Libby closed the blind and stepped over one of the moving boxes that she had packed before dinner. She had to make her move now. There was no more reason to wait, and she felt that things were becoming more physically dangerous. She had already been kidnapped and brutalized, suspiciously found by Jacob and her parents, and then electrocuted. And Captain Smith's sudden interest and presence was also raising her suspicions.

She had had the moving boxes stored in a closet in anticipation of this very day. Libby had been a minimalist the whole time that she was in Atheneum, so there was not much that she had to pack. Ever since she received that letter in college that told her to only worry about the bare minimum, she kept up that practice of living light. She had not known when she would have to move quickly again.

Next to her bed was a suitcase with a sufficient amount of clothing and items that she was going to be needing with her. She had arranged for movers to come in the morning and pack whatever she still had left out, and from there, they would be taking all her belongings to Minnesota. Libby had no plans of returning to the cottage after she left the courthouse. She wanted to be long gone from Atheneum by the next sundown, and Texas itself by the following sunrise.

Libby had already brought out everything from the floorboards earlier in the evening; all of the cash and paperwork that she had stored there. She would be taking these precious papers to the probate office at the courthouse tomorrow. After that, she would drive out of the horrible town with people that had done nothing but agonize and plague her for more than two years.

Libby knew that if she could fall asleep by 4 a.m., she could sleep for four hours. The courthouse did not open until 9 a.m., giving her an ample forty-five minutes to get ready beforehand. Even though she would climb into bed and attempt to fall asleep, she knew that she her mind was too wound up, and all of the many thoughts running through her head of tomorrow's events would keep her from drifting off.

***

There was no one else in the probate office when Libby walked in. She had moved quickly after exiting her car, not bothering to look around at anything or anyone. She hoped that the process that she was coming here for would not take long, and she could be on her way — never having the need to have her head on a swivel again.

Libby pulled out her needed paperwork from the folder in her hand. Before she had taken barely two steps toward the employee sitting behind the glass partition at the counter, Libby felt the breeze from the door as it opened up forcefully behind her, and heard the loud thump against the wall as it slammed into it.

"Libby, stop right now," she heard before she had even gotten a chance to turn around to the commotion. Right away, she knew whose voice it was behind her, but couldn't understand why he was there. She started towards the counter again, disregarding his words, as well as the slightly frightened look on the face of the clerk before her.

"If you hand those papers over to that clerk, I will not be able to help you, Libby," the voice gave another warning. "You still have a chance."

Libby flung around and screamed, "I'm not doing anything wrong! And stop calling me Libby, Joshua! My real name is Penny Schickle, and I am only claiming what is mine!"

"No, Libby. You are not Penny," Captain Smith said, remaining calm. "Please just stop now. You can get out from under this."

"I am telling you that my name is Penny Schickle, and I am getting the land that my mother was going to inherit and then pass down to me!" Libby huffed before movement made her avert her attention to the door. She took a step back when she saw Jacob through the glass slit. He hesitated before he turned the knob and entered.

"Libby," was all that he said before the two of them spent about thirty seconds staring at each other.

"Jacob told me everything," Captain Smith said, breaking the silence.

"What does he know?" Libby asked, still looking at Jacob. "He is no one."

"Hummmmp," Jacob sounded, and gave Libby a satisfied smirk. "I know plenty. You left me in your dorm room more than once after your genealogy project. Your parents had been so concerned and so adamant for me to stop you from turning in your project, that I had to find out what the big deal was. They would not give me any solid or specific details, so I went through and read anything that I could find in your dorm room. I eventually came across the very interesting paperwork that you are probably holding in your hands right now.

"I saw what plans your Mom had. I read all of the newspaper articles about what happened. Not just what you had, but I also did plenty of my own research. I know that twenty years ago, your mother's roommate from college, Amelia, along with her daughter Penny, came from Atheneum to Louisiana to visit her. But your Mom claimed that Amelia never made it. She says that she was at the train station to pick her up, but the two of them never got off the train. But we know what your parents did to Amelia. And her daughter Penny, too, for that matter."

"No," Libby said. "You got it all wrong. They did nothing to Penny! I am Penny! Lorelei and Nathaniel raised me as their own daughter! Lorelei had to have a daughter so that she could claim the land. The Sleuth land. So she kept me."

Jacob shook his head, and gave Libby a pitying look. "If that were true, then why did she change the paperwork to say that the land would be hers and hers only? Why wasn't her plan to bequeath the land to you, as Amelia's original documents said that she would be passing the land along to Penny?"

Since Libby only glared at him, and did not answer, Jacob continued. "That is because she just wanted to sell the land and have the money from it. She cared nothing about preserving the history of the land, and keep it being passed on. She is just a conniver that is only out for her own personal gain. And apparently, you have inherited those same conniving genes from her."

"No, I have not," Libby said. "There is no way that I could have, because she is not my mother!

"Yes, she is," Jacob said, "And you know that for a fact, as well as Nathaniel being your father. They are both your very own, very real, biological parents."

"And these are the lies that you've decided to tell Joshua here?" Libby looked at Captain Smith. "You didn't believe any of this rubbish, did you?"

Captain Smith moved away and stood with his back against the wall.

Jacob continued, "In some kind of way, you found that forged paperwork that she had drawn up. She had already stolen the real documents from Amelia when she had gone to Atheneum one time to visit her. Amelia had the paperwork in a desk drawer. She probably never even thought that she couldn't trust guests in her home and needed to have that type of paperwork locked up.

"But Lorelei needed to get rid of her before Amelia discovered that the papers were missing, giving her a chance to report it and have new ones drawn up."

"But it was only Amelia," Libby said. "Not Penny. Not me. Just Amelia! What other reason would they have for making me have that surgery to erase my memory. That way I would not remember my real mother Lorelei." Stumbling, she said, "I mean, I mean Amelia."

"I believe you accidentally witnessed the tragic ordeal with poor Amelia and Penny and that is why your parents had you have the surgery," Jacob provided. "You probably got up out of bed, went wandering and saw it. Those dreams that you had when you were young explain it. Even down to the name."

"What name?" Libby asked.

"Melanie," Jacob told her. "That name Melanie."

"What about it? About her?" Just like when he was at her house a few weeks ago, Jacob peaked Libby's curiosity. Although she was irritated that he and Captain Smith were there, she also couldn't help wanting to know exactly how much he knew.

"Occasionally, Amelia's husband called her Melly. You probably heard that a time or two, but misconstrued it as Melanie in your dreams. It only makes sense to think that you must have seen what happened to Amelia."

Libby waited a few seconds before answering. "That summation is conveniently logical, Jacob. Everything just fits into place. Do you really think that dream is about something that actually took place? That's too easy."

"Oh. I'm not nearly done."

"There's no need to say more," Libby said before turning to look at Captain Smith. She decided that she really didn't want Jacob to say more. At this point, with everything that had already been said, the clerk was likely to be hesitant to accept Libby's paperwork, and start the process of her taking ownership of the Sleuth land.

"This is ludicrous," Libby said. "The two of you can just leave, so that I can finish my business and be on my way." She turned back to face the counter and the clerk who stood mesmerized. Libby felt like she would look perfect if she was holding and eating a tub of popcorn.

Jacob disregarded Libby's request, as though he was determined to say everything that he had come to say. "It has already been twenty years since Amelia disappeared. The more time that went by would have worked in your mother's favor, because people very often commented that Lorelei and Amelia looked very much alike. After all of that time, change in a person's appearance would be expected. Your mother was going to come back and claim to be Amelia, and say that she left Atheneum and her husband due to abuse."

Libby turned to Jacob again and yelled, "Stop calling her my mother!"

Even with Libby's outburst, Jacob's determination did not falter. "With the exception of one person, no one else around here would be able to say for certain that it wasn't really Amelia, not even the childhood friends that she grew up with. She could easily brush off their stories from growing up, and say that she forgot them. But she wasn't planning any reunions. I'm sure that she only anticipated being in Atheneum to claim the land, and quickly sell it without showing her face too much.

"Instead, she was most likely going to wait until Poppy was no longer here. Since Amelia was his daughter, he is the only one that would really know that Lorelei was a fraud. Lorelei would not have been able to pull the wool over his eyes and say that she forgot things about her childhood growing up with him in Atheneum. Especially since it was going to involve something such as valuable as that Sleuth land. No one else except for Poppy would have really cared."

"You had to bring him up, huh?" Libby sneered. "What? Is he also waiting outside, ready to come in and try to take this away from me as well?"

"No, Libby," Jacob said, sounding saddened. "Poppy has been hurt enough by this. There is nothing that he could gain by being here. Only heartbreak by looking into your face knowing what you are trying to do."

That statement made Libby turn her face away from Jacob's before he continued talking. "I know that he told you about the famous founding families of Atheneum. And definitely told you about Miriam, one of the last Sleuths that had been left in the area after many tragedies and other circumstances. She was indeed with child when George Sleuth moved her away, and the child she had was named Cassandra.

"Why am I even telling you this. You know it all. You are well aware that Poppy met and married Cassandra Peck elsewhere, but they decided to live and raise a family in Atheneum. Cassandra was enamored by the way Miriam and George talked about the place, and she felt like that is where she belonged. With Miriam's one-of-a-kind personality, she also had no qualms talking to Cassandra about the Jades — in particular, her father Charles Jade."

"And yada-yada," Libby interjected. "To Atheneum they went, they had Amelia, she grew up and went to Wellesley College in Boston, Lorelei was her roommate for two of those years, and fast-forward, Lorelei did what she did to Amelia. Blah, blah, blah."

Jacob sneered at Libby once she said, "Fast forward some more, and I am now here for my land inheritance."

"How far do you think that you would have made it if Captain Smith and I had not come here today?" Jacob asked her.

She looked over at Captain Smith who was still standing against the wall. She had practically forgotten that he was there in those last moments.

When she did not answer that, Jacob said, "You would have gotten nowhere Libby. That's where. Do you think you could have just walked in here today, file some papers, and then one day walk out with the deed to the land?"

"Of course I did, being that it is my land," she answered.

Jacob huffed loudly. "And you and your family are supposed to be so smart." In a condescending tone, he added, "You do realize that DNA testing would definitely be done, right? That's something Aunt Lorelei probably didn't think through twenty years ago. I'm sure that greed was the only thing on her mind." He snickered before adding, "Some doctor."

Libby was coming to full realization that her plans would not be coming to fruition. Not that day, and not any day. As the seconds passed, and she continued to stare at Jacob, her blood started to simmer. Her chest began heaving right before she lunged toward him.

Jacob closed his eyes and put his arms up in front of him in defense, his hands blocking his face. He likely expected to feel hits or punches against his body. Once there were none, he slowly opened his eyes and saw why. In Captain Smith's hand was the paperwork that Libby had come there with. After he stopped reading one of the pages, he pushed Libby face first into the same wall that he had been leaning against.

"Libby Ferguson, you are under arrest for the possession of stolen property," he informed her. "You have the right to remain silent."

"Joshua no! What are you doing!" Libby screamed. "I didn't even turn the papers in! Just ... just like you said."

"Anything you say can and will be used against you in a court of law," Captain Smith continued, while placing handcuffs on Libby's wrists. "You have a right to an attorney. If you cannot afford an attorney, one will be appointed for you." He gripped Libby's left arm and pulled her away from the wall, using his free hand to open the door.

"No, Josh!" she was again screaming. "No! Don't do this!"

Captain Smith handed Libby off to another police officer that had been waiting in the hallway. "She's all yours," he said.

Libby turned her head back as much as she could after that officer began leading her outside. She yelled at Captain Smith, "This is how you're helping me? This is how I'm getting from under it?"

By the time the officer had gotten to his police car with Libby, tears had already been flowing from her eyes. She had not paid attention to any of the people that were around while she was being escorted away from the court building. But once she was seated and locked in the back seat of the police car, she looked out of the window, and observed the area.

She had to blink quite a few times, and only got rid of some of the blur, but she knew that her eyes were not deceiving her. Jacob was being led by Captain Smith to his own police car.

In handcuffs.

Chapter Twenty
by Lakisha Sparrow

2019

"What other crime fiction books would you recommend?" Libby was asked by a pert teenager with a big smile plastered on her face.

Libby signed the title page of the book that the girl handed her, and gave it back to her. "Unfortunately, I only read one book like that, just to get me prepared for writing this novel," she responded. "Otherwise, there was just the how-to book that I utilized to help me. As you may have noticed, this type of fiction is not the genre that I have written in previously."

"Yes. I was a little thrown off by it at first. But your other books were so good, I decided to give it a shot. I hadn't ever read this type of book in my life, but you have made me want more,

more, more, of them," the girl said, still beaming.

"Well now that I know for sure that I have at least one true fan, I may have to write some more like this," Libby said before the girl thanked her and left.

Libby was at the last stop of her book tour, ending a full year run this time. The first book tour that she had gone on was only six months long, and started about five months after she was released from prison. Libby had served fifteen months of a eighteen month sentence, during which time she wrote two trilogies, and three standalone novels. After her release, she went straight to the task of self-publishing those books.

Once she generated some income from the sales of those, along with financial help from her brother Richard, Libby was confident enough to go on tour. Since she was experienced in the publishing industry, she did not have the fear of going on tour alone. She had known that some new authors feel like a book signing is like throwing a party and being certain no one will come. They opt to go on tour with other authors that they feel are going through the same agony as them, lessening the feeling of looking lost and amateurish all by themselves.

The nine books that she written while incarcerated were all paranormal and fantasy fiction books. Since Libby was limited in having access to research during that time, she had to use to her imagination to create content, and those two genres worked out perfectly for her.

    While Libby was on her first tour, she utilized her spare time to research and write the novel that she was currently on tour for. If she had a signing during the evening, she researched during the day. If her mornings or afternoons were booked, she spent nights poring over whatever she could find about the Amelia Schickle case, and Atheneum itself. Libby chose to ride intercity buses and trains between cities on her tour, just so that she would have time to write while traveling.

    While she had previously wanted to visit the museum in Atheneum to do research and write a fictional novel about her experiences in the town, it didn't work out that way. At least not exactly. While Libby still wound up writing a book about Atheneum, it wasn't the same as what she previously said she was going to do. Instead of her experiences, she wrote about Amelia's life there, and the aftermath of her disappearance. Of course that meant that she had to write about her own life, and that of her parents. She was fine with doing that, and was pleased that she finally was able to find out more about both of her parents' lineage — their real family and upbringing.

    Because of Libby's success with the other books she wrote, she was able to have her current book released through a traditional publishing company. She was happy for that since she had written a book that was different from the others, and didn't want the solitary task of convincing her first audience to follow her to a different genre.

However, she was unhappy that the company insisted that she had to have a book signing in Atheneum, or at least somewhere near there. They told her that it would be befitting, and there would likely be a large turnout of people in the town of which the book is based.
Libby adamantly refused, and was lucky that there were no bookstores in Atheneum that were prominent or large enough for a book signing event. She informed them that when she worked at HouBayou, the company always rented a ballroom at a hotel or such for their signings.

The publishing company and Libby worked out a compromise instead — and it was where she currently was. The decision had been to have the event at Lone Star Bookstore in Tomball, which at first was not a much better plan, because she was still very close to Atheneum.

There were very few people besides her coworkers that Libby had known by name when she lived there. However, there had been plenty of familiar faces throughout the night, and she cringed each time one came to have their book signed. But after a while she began to relax. She had gotten nothing but positive comments, and everyone that she conversed with stated that they were happy that she wrote the book, and were pleased that justice was served.

Libby made it to the end of the book signing and began to pack up her items once she felt that no one else was there for an autograph. Her head was down as she reached for the last book on the table, so all she saw was a wizened hand that grabbed it before she did. But then a small figure bounded into her view, followed by an excited greeting that momentarily paralyzed Libby in place.

"Miss Libby!"

It was Ruthie.

Accompanied by Poppy.

Of course.

"Heir within a jade," he said, tracing the title with the index finger on his left hand. He then used the same hand to give the front cover of the book a weak thump. "From what I've heard, this is one astounding book."

Libby lifted her head, recovering from the shock of the sudden presence before her. She looked into Poppy's face, and braced herself for whatever he planned to say or do to her. Out of all of the people that she had been worried about encountering at the event, Grant T. Uldrich was by far the one person that she had ultimately feared would show up.

"It wouldn't be fair if you ran off without signing a copy for me, would it?" Poppy said. "I think that I might even have a place in this novel."

"Poppy said that we would come here, and I could have hot chocolate while he had coffee with a friend," Ruthie reported. "I didn't know that he was talking about you. I haven't seen you in like forever! Where you been, Miss Libby?"

Libby looked at her and thought about her answer. She considered saying that she was on a long vacation, or that she had moved. While the latter was true, technically, Libby just decided not to respond to the question at all. She instead feigned excitement and exclaimed, "You are really growing Miss Ruthie! You will be as tall as me soon!"

"Yep! I've been eating my spinach and doing gymnastics," Ruthie said with an enthusiasm that matched Libby's. "I think it's working."

Libby kept looking at Ruthie, but Libby did not know what else to say to her. Poppy ultimately broke the silence.

"Well, Libby," he said. "How about it. Won't you please join us for coffee and hot chocolate?"

Libby looked at Poppy, but again couldn't make any words come out of her mouth.

Poppy seemed to understand that she was uncomfortable, and tried to lighten the mood. "My treat," he added.

Libby turned toward her belongings, and finally spoke. "Actually, I'm done here. I'm all packed up to leave," she said, and turned back to face him.

Poppy opened his mouth to say something, but then stopped. He turned to his granddaughter and put his hand on her shoulder. "Go ahead up into the cafe, Ruthie," he told her. "Libby and I will be right behind you. Get us a nice table."

"Okay," Ruthie said before bounding away to her duty.

In a soft voice, Poppy said, "I mean you no harm, Libby. Please just sit with me for few minutes. We may never get another chance to talk to each other."

Libby hesitated a little more, but then picked up her purse, and started walking toward the cafe. Poppy followed closely behind, and they climbed the steps to the split level in which it was located. They joined Ruthie at the table she had chosen along the edge. From there one could see very well into other areas of the bookstore. The Children's section was right below on the left, and Ruthie very well had noticed it.

"Poppy," she said and jumped up from her chair before Poppy or Libby had a chance to sit down. "Can I just have my hot chocolate later? I want to go look at some books." She began pointing through the railing and told him, "You can see me right down there the whole time."

Poppy looked at the area that she was referring to and said, "I think that that will be a mighty fine idea. Miss Libby and I do have some boring stuff to talk about that you probably don't want to hear. But we will be sure to watch you from here."

"Yea!" she squealed and quickly left. Poppy and Libby sat down once they were certain that they had a good view of her.

Neither of them spoke for the next few minutes. They avoided looking at each other — the pair just scanned their surroundings, and also watched Ruthie.

Eventually, Poppy told Libby, "I sensed that you were apprehensive to speak to me. So I'll start off by letting you know one thing."

Libby stared at her hands that were folded and resting on the table in front of her. She could not bring herself to look up at Poppy while sitting that close at the table with him.

"I forgive you, Libby," he said. "I need you to know that."

She continued looking at her hands, and Poppy let a few moments pass before speaking again. "I know what greed does to people, and I understand how it may have been so easy for you to be motivated by that. I don't think that you were necessarily moving from a malicious standpoint."

Libby thought back to the genealogy project and how she felt weeks later when she got the DNA results back from the items that she gathered during that Thanksgiving break. When she first found the paperwork and information in the safe that week, she thought that maybe she finally had the answer to why her mother had never been warm to her while growing up. When she first saw the paperwork and articles with the missing mother and daughter, her first thoughts were, *"Maybe that's why my mom has always been so distant from me. We're not biologically connected. The will says that the heir would need to have a daughter in order to be bequeated the Sleuth land. I'm probably Amelia's missing daughter that Lorelei stole and raised after getting rid of Amelia."* Libby thought she understood everything at that point.

But instead, the DNA results that she received made it conclusive that Nathaniel and Lorelei Ferguson were her true and biological parents. It angered Libby to know that her mother had been distant and uncaring towards her for no apparent reason. She topped that with finding the forgeries that Lorelei had made did not benefit Libby at all. None of the inheritance would have gone to her. That is when Libby decided that she would beat her mother at her own game and take the inheritance from her. So Libby forged the forgeries, and decided to claim that she was Amelia's missing daughter, Penny.

Sitting at the bookstore cafe with Poppy, however, she was not going to disagree with him and let him know that it was indeed malice that motivated her to do what she did.

Although she still did not look at Poppy, in a voice barely above a whisper she said, "Yes, that's true. But it's not like I needed the money from the sale of the land. My parents had provided well for me my entire life."

She waited several seconds, and then Libby finally raised her head and looked at Poppy. He said, "That may be. But you don't get to be my age without learning a few things. And one thing I know is, if one is presented with a substantial monetary gain, and they believe that they can get away with it, it is not far-fetched that they might try to do just that."

Libby put her head down again before saying, "You are definitely right about that," she said. "I did recently spend a lot of time with people who thought that very thing." Not one of the other prisoners that she met while incarcerated had stated that they knew that they were going to get caught, and that they wanted to be there.

Now that Libby was thrust into thinking about her time there, her body and mind went into that mode. The constant, nagging aura around the prisoners that silently told them that they always needed to be on alert, and show confidence, even to the point of putting fear in others, was suddenly upon her.

Libby raised her head and spoke in an assured manner and tone. "There are questions that I have for you, *Poppy*," she said, adding emphasis on his name in a way that suggested she had a problem with it, or that she hated having to utter it.

"When I first met you at the ball, why did you tell me that the state owned that Sleuth land, when it was you that had legal ownership of it as the compulsory heir after your wife's death, and Amelia's disappearance? she asked.

"I said that just to gauge your reaction," he said, looking back at her in the same manner that he had been already, giving no regard to her sudden change in her demeanor.

"So you knew then who I was, and what I was up to?" Libby asked, a sharp tone now in her voice.

"I did not know why exactly, but as soon as you came to town, someone had put a bug in my ear and told me that you were trouble, and that I needed to watch you. But in all that time you were here, you didn't do anything, and I didn't really know what I was supposed to be watching. I barely ever thought about it anymore.

"And then, because of Ruthie, you coincidentally wound up at my table at the ball. I took that chance to see what the trouble was." He paused before adding, "I knew I had to act quick, though, but I didn't even know what approach to take. I finally just decided to mention things about the town and the people and see if I could get a bite.

"There was a time that the state really did have control of it. As you of course know Libby, my wife Cassandra had already passed away before Amelia met her awful date with your parents. Once Amelia disappeared, the last thing that I was thinking about was that land. I just let it rot. I cared nothing about that when I had been left all alone and hurting inside. My wife was a Sleuth, and this just fell in line with all of the other hexes that the family seemed to be plagued with.

"Most of the town — well pretty much just the Jades — wanted me to leave after Cassandra and Amelia were gone. They felt that there was no reason that I would need to stay here since I was not connected in the familial sense anymore. But I was not going to let them push me out. Unfortunately, Amelia's husband didn't have the same tenacity as I had, and he did move away. He didn't want to be in his house without his wife and daughter, in a town where he wasn't wanted.

"At first I thought I was staying in case Amelia ever called or showed back up. But there was something that I did a few years later that forced me to realize that that was not the reason that I stayed in Atheneum," he said.

"And what was that? Libby asked.

"Well," he started, but then paused. He looked up at the ceiling before continuing. "I like to call it a short-term escapade, but some people have other names for it. And since it so happened to involve a Jade ... that just upped the scandal level so much more. My actions proved to me that I was really just staying around to spite them.

"I wound up having Bonnie as the result of my deeds, but her mother unfortunately was embarrassed out of town. And that was by her own family. But no matter how they felt about me, or what they said to me, they were not going to run me away. So stay I did.

"That's part of the reason that Brandon and Wilson were extra physical with me during that ordeal we had with them that weekend. I know they felt like they were defending the family honor and name for what I did to sully one of them. The two of them pretty much reminded me of the Keystone Cops in their antics that day," he ended, and gave a small chuckle. But the smile that accompanied it quickly faded, and Poppy got a faraway look in his eyes that he held for several seconds.

Libby figured that he was probably replaying scenes of that weekend in his head, just as she had done many times since then. Poppy kept her from doing that again right then, however, because he started speaking again.

"Yeah. It's very humorous to me." He scoffed, smiled again and added, "Now."

They became quiet again, and Libby began to ruminate. She figured that since she was sitting here with him, she may as well compare stories with Poppy about her cousin Jacob. She thought back to one of Richard's visits early in her incarceration, when he told her that he had gone to visit Jacob while he had also been imprisoned.

Libby had looked forward to Richard's visits, but she was livid when her brother mentioned that, and she slammed her hands on the table. She was poised to push off at the elbows, get up and leave the table, and return to her lonely cell.

Before she could even do that however, Richard was able to stop her. They weren't allowed to touch each other, so he forcefully, yet quietly told her, "Calm down."

Libby glared at him, strongly exhaled, then slowly removed her hands from the table. She realized at once that she had been haste in her actions, and was glad that her brother had stopped her. As it stood, he was barely able to visit her once a month. He, of course, was her only visitor, and she did not want to anger him and lose that.

"Think about it Libby," he started to explain. "First some police officers come to the house and haul Mom and Dad away in handcuffs. Then I get a call from you telling me that you're also in jail, and you think I didn't want to find out what it was all about?

"I know what you had told me, and I know what Mom and Dad had told me when I had visited them at their facilities as well. You all had different stories in the beginning, and I knew that none of you were telling me everything. Now that you have all been to trial, I have answers about this whole, unfortunate mess. But before that, I wanted to hear what Jacob had to say, and see what his part was in this. I needed to know — because there was no logical explanation as to how he fit into this crime from so many years ago."

Up until that point, Libby had been unaware of what Jacob's fate had been. But Richard let her know that Jacob had only been sentenced to serve five months in jail, and that he had been convicted of "Misprision of Felony."

"Prosecutions for that crime are practically nonexistent," her brother informed her, "but the Jades used their influence to exact some kind of punishment for Jacob, even if only for a short period. And this was despite him actually being the one that did report the incident to the police in the first place."

It hadn't made sense to Libby, however, and she pondered to Richard, "Amelia was a Sleuth, though. Why would the Jades care about getting justice for her?"

Richard laughed and said, "They didn't care about that or her at all. Which is unfortunate when you think about it in the humane and compassionate sense, but still worked out anyway. The Jades only did it because they were not happy with Jacob playing both ends against the middle. And to make matters worse, he did that in two separate ways. It was our parents and you opposing each other, as well as Poppy and the Jades opposing each other. He was in the middle of both sets, looking for what he could gain. Once it became obvious that he did not stand to gain from anyone, he decided to be a hero and admit his knowledge.

"He told me that he expected to get off scot-free, too, since he provided the information about what happened. But by golly, the Jades were not having it," Richard said while shaking his head. "I have learned a lot about that family in these past few months."

"I've been so lost about so much this whole time," Libby informed her brother. "And that whole time, it was Jacob that had all of the answers?" She asked the question more to herself than her brother, but he still answered.

"Yes. Jacob was in control of a lot — basically all of it," Richard said. "That investment deal you did with his friend? That return money you received came from our parents. They told him to find a way to get you out of the way. So he set it all up. He got the money deposited, and he finagled and maneuvered to get you that contract position at the publishing company that you had been working for, even though you didn't technically meet the qualifications. And he knew how much it would irk Mom and Dad that he had you in Atheneum — the very last place that they would want you to be. He brought you right to the big ole prize that so many different people seem to want — that Sleuth land."

During that visit, Richard's revelations from Jacob did answer a lot of questions for Libby. Everything just fell into place — including the night that he showed up at the establishment in which Libby was celebrating her birthday, and she discovered him talking to Poppy in the men's restroom. It clearly explained why Jacob was with Wilson and Brandon after she and Poppy had been kidnapped and held hostage. It explained how and why her parents showed up to her hotel after she escaped the kidnapping.

It was all Jacob. Jacob. Jacob.

He was a great actor throughout the entire performance. When he was at her house that morning on her birthday, and he pretended that he did not know anything about why she left college and ended up in Atheneum.

It was all Jacob. Jacob. Jacob.

When he found her in the woods after she escaped from the library, he lamented about how hard life had been for him as he took on an air of innocence and docility to plead his case that day.

It was all Jacob. Jacob. Jacob.

But as Libby still sat there in the bookstore with Poppy, she ultimately decided against bringing Jacob into the conversation. She did not really need to know from Poppy whether or not his story matched with what her brother Richard had told her.

Yet it still bugged her to know one thing after all of this time, so she posed an alternate question to Poppy instead.

"Who is Sammy Sleuth?"

Poppy laughed and said, "Is that what you have been thinking about all of this time that you have been sitting here, lost in thought, saying nothing?"

"Yes," Libby lied.

Poppy looked at her, and she knew that he was aware that she been thinking about a lot more than that name that he had thrown out during the kidnapping.

"Well," he advised, in a chastising tone that could suggest that she had not paid attention throughout the whole time that she had been embroiled in the entire Atheneum and Sleuth land ordeal. "Like I have pretty much already said – Wilson and Brandon are idiots."

***

Libby managed to finally leave the bookstore, and the uncomfortable conversation and presence of being with Poppy. She said goodbye to the both him and Ruthie, while giving an awkward hug to him, and a warm and genuine one to Ruthie.

Before the two of them left the table, however, she had asked Poppy what had become of the situation with his daughter Bonnie. Since Libby did her research from afar, it was something that she had never uncovered while writing the novel about Amelia and Atheneum.

Poppy explained that it was Bonnie herself that had set up and carried out the incident on the train tracks. He told Libby, "She had always had an inferiority complex when it came to Amelia. She grew up watching me grieve about her sister, and she has expressed to me more than once that there was an ominous cloud over me that was never going to go away. Add to that her feelings about being born under a different type of circumstance, and the fact that her mother left her with me."

He shook his head and looked at towards the floor. "I think that once you came around, she may have overheard conversations between Jacob and me, or even found out something from Brandon or Wilson. She never said anything specific, but she knew that there was something going on that had to do with the Sleuth land and Amelia, and said that she had had enough. She came up with a way to leave the gloom."

Now it made sense to Libby why Bonnie was so venomous to her in their encounters. "Well it sounds like you are saying that she did return to town," Libby said to him as she stood up to leave. With a tone of enmity she added, "And her daughter."

After Poppy confirmed that Bonnie did return to Atheneum, his story gave Libby the realization that Bonnie's actions had been susceptible to become a situation of déjà vu — had she stayed away. She would have been another daughter of Poppy's that mysteriously disappeared, and Ruthie would have been another daughter in Poppy's life that had been left by her mother.

The thought of history repeating itself chilled Libby enough to shudder once she was away from Poppy. She did not want to imagine reliving her time in Atheneum, and was glad that her business at the bookstore was over. Once Libby had been forced to come to Tomball for the book signing, she knew that this was the perfect opportunity to go to the bank to finally withdraw the money that had been deposited for her by Jacob. After she had been released from prison, she steered clear of the Atheneum area, and also did not necessarily want any parts of the money that was so ill-gotten to her. But now that she was here, she wanted this to be her last visit to either of the two towns forever.

    She was planning to stay at Jardin del Verde hotel for the night, before going to the bank the next morning. But instead of going straight to the hotel to get a room, she decided to drive to the Sleuth land to sit and reflect on the entity that caused such turmoil in her life.

    She drove to the site and at first thought that her eyes were deceiving her, or that she had simply forgotten how to get to the correct place. But once she had gotten out of her car and walked toward a huge sign planted in the ground, she realized that she was indeed in the correct place. Even from quite a distance in the dark she was able to read what it said:

Sleuth Memorial Park
Opens at Dawn
Closes at Dusk

Libby took a quick scan of the area, and her eyes fell on something that told her that she was not going to be staying there to look around or sit thinking about anything at all. Because there, parked in an inconspicuous corner, was Atheneum police car number 1030.

She quickly returned to her rental car and drove away from the park. She checked her rearview mirror several times and was grateful that she never saw the reflection of headlights following her on the dark road leading out.

Once she made it to the hotel, she remained in the parking lot and searched for information on her cell phone. She looked up the website of the airline that she was slated to leave with the following day, to see if there were any flights that she could get on in the next few hours.

When she found a flight that was leaving in three hours, there was nothing but screeching tire sounds leaving the parking lot as her car headed to Bush-Intercontinental Airport.

Biographies

Over the years, numerous people have told Lakisha that she should write a novel. So far, she has not been able to commit to that task. She occasionally dabbles in Camp NaNoWriMo, and maybe one day her friends and family will see a complete story to fruition.

Lakisha came across a model of this writing project, and knew that she had to put together one of her own. In addition to facilitating all aspects of the venture, she also edited the entire novel.

Lakisha is from Long Island, NY, and currently lives in Spring, TX. When she is not parenting her three miniature stories at home, she spends her other waking hours in her favorite place of all time — the library.

Ollie Bream unwittingly signed up to be the youngest member of the Tomball Community Writing Project, but that didn't frighten her in the least. Ollie loves to read all kinds of books in her spare time, including Harry Potter, The Little Prince, and Red Rising. She often writes as well, but can never get past a short story. She is excited to announce that Chapter Two is her first public work outside of submitting a story to the Scholastic Writing Contest.

Ollie currently resides in Tomball, TX, but has moved not only around the country, but also the world - from Tennessee to Australia. You can often find her losing miserably at a game of Putt-Putt with her friends.

Originally from the East Coast, 'L' spent most of her childhood in Houston. She has worked as a secretary, waitress, actress, counselor, newspaper reporter, stand-up comedienne, and joke writer. Her writing has been selected for Rice University's Glasscock School of Continuing Studies Writers' Gallery, published in both local and national publications, and earned awards in various Texas and Oklahoma writing groups. A member of *Sisters in Crime*, and a bookseller with Barnes & Noble since 2007, L's favorite book recommendations fall in the Domestic Psychological Suspense category. 'L' has a humorous mystery in the editing stage, but she's most excited about the manuscript she hopes to finish this year — a novel of dark, psychological suspense.

When 'L' is not working at the bookstore or thinking up a scene for her novel, she enjoys: walks with her husband and their rescue dogs, laughing at Tonight Show episodes with her brother, and dreaming of visits to her wonderful step-children and grandchildren.

Elizabeth reads. And reads. And reads. A lot.

Sometimes she writes. A little.

When she saw the advertisement for the Tomball Community Writing Project, she thought that maybe this would be a catalyst to force herself to write more. So far, her previous writing has just been for personal reflection and enjoyment, but Elizabeth was happy to branch out and make a public contribution to this project. She is looking forward to continue in her writing endeavors, and you may see more of her writing in future submissions.

Genova Boyd has been writing on and off for many years both personally and professionally. She is a blogger and an aspiring novelist, and has also written academically. Coming from Sydney, Australia, she has picked up a couple of History degrees, a teaching degree, and a Masters in Library Science. She has also traveled a fair bit, and loves taking photographs of her journeys for writing reference. She is a regular face at the Lone Star College-Tomball Community Library (you can find her at the Reference Desk), and can be seen scouring websites, author pages, and conferences for new and upcoming books.

When she saw the Community Writing Project, Genova thought it would be fun to contribute to a book that could go anywhere. When she's not at the library, Genova is at home with her husband, child, and two dogs — usually hiding somewhere and working on her own novel.

Stephanie works many hours a week as a paramedic, and that allows her to be a part of some very colorful lives. She is working on a series of novels featuring different first-responders, and their intertwining lives with medical staff at a local hospital.

In the meantime, Stephanie enjoys many travels with her children in the US and abroad, and maintains a travel blog to chronicle their adventures. She has contributed to *Houston Family Magazine*, as well as *W Magazine*. You can find her walking her dogs around Tomball, planning out the locations to be featured in her novels.

Maria Christina Yardas is from the beautiful country, Philippines, and now lives in Spring, Texas. She has worked as a nanny, restaurant staff, and other interesting jobs to help her family.

The Tomball Community Writing Project was a dream come true for her because she loves to write stories and songs. Her affinity for writing started when she was in high school playing with paper dolls. She loved to write down the scripts instead of just making them up as she went along. When she was approached to become a part of this project, she was excited and scared at the same time. English is her second language, and she took advantage of the help that Tomball Community Library and others on the writing team provided to develop her chapter into its special place in the novel.

Most of the time she stays at home playing and reading stories with her daughter, and that makes her life wonderful.

Osiria Kage has been writing since she was a child, and has won a few awards through writing competitions. She is currently in the process of writing her first novel, *Marionette*.

Osiria was still in high school when she wrote her chapter, and then began her first year of college as a Creative Writing major. Writing is a passion that she hopes to make a career of in the future.

Mickie is originally from Pennsylvania, but has been enjoying a nomadic lifestyle for about four years. She's been writing since she was a child and learned about NaNoWriMo when she was in high school. Since 2010, she has participated in every NaNo, being awarded several years in a row.

One of her main goals during high school was to self-publish a book — which she did complete. While taking classes at Lone Star College-Tomball, she learned about and joined this writing project. As of late, she's been pursuing Journalism and living near Dallas, Texas, after taking a hiatus for the summer to visit the Western countryside.

My name is Ann James and I live in Kingwood, Texas with my husband and three dogs. I love to read and write, and I have completed three novels which haven't been published—yet! I am forever hopeful.

Currently, I'm working on a fourth novel and a children's book based on the adventures of my dog, Willow. She is a therapy dog and has some wonderful tales to tell.

There is generally a gentle sound of canine snoring underfoot while CS is working. Ergo, coffee. The tension between sleep and caffeine forms the backbone of CS's writing, along with frequent walks through Mercer Arboretum to enjoy the Texas sunshine (or Texas cloudiness, especially in the summer).

A poet and short story writer, CS maintains a blog at *Moon Pools and Mermaids* for current projects and inspirations. She has published a book of Poetry, *Blue Coconut Days*, and is currently working on a novel.

Jesus Galvan was a late recruit to the Tomball Community Writing Project. He read several of the chapters of the novel, and thought it would be fun to take part in the creation. He was not sure if there would still be a spot for him since the project was already well underway, but he was glad that he asked. Jesus is also proud that he is the first male writer to be featured in the project.

Jesus has not been published professionally yet, but it is something that he would like to happen in the future.

Alpana Sarangapani is a Reference Librarian at Lone Star College-Tomball Community Library. She enjoys working, helping, and sharing information with people.

She believes that "Life is a school of learning." She enjoys writing stories (not many have read them), and to work as part of a team, so this was a perfect project for her.

Christie Gray

I am a lover of words, a single mother of three grown children and a doghter. I am a handler of books, and dark roasted coffee beans. I am finally settling down enough to spend some time writing, and hope to have more to show for it in the next five years. Creatively, my favorite genres to write are Romance and Christian Fiction.

Shontrell Wade is a freelance editor and self-proclaimed book addict. She has edited a range of literary genres from urban fiction to traditional romance and fantasy, articles and papers written by undergraduate and graduate students, as well as business documents of all types. Besides writing her own newspaper and magazine articles, Shontrell also maintains a blog about authors and books.

Shontrell joined the Tomball Community Writing Project once she was ready to take a break from the editing side of writing and get back into the trenches of creating a story.

Patrick G Howard is famous for adding a pinch of embellishment and a dash humor to turn a good story into a classic, which is why it's hard to believe that the Tomball Community Writing Project was his first attempt at writing fiction. He enjoyed adding his unique style to the project, and hopes that you will enjoy it too.

Patrick is a popular speaker and writer of non-fiction, mostly inspirational and spiritual topics. He is a lifelong Texan and resides in Tomball. His occupation is a mortgage loan officer, and he loves seeing the look of joy on people's faces when they get the keys to their new home.

In his spare time, Patrick loves to perform music. He is an accomplished musician and has taken the stage as a percussionist with some of Houston's finest symphonic ensembles. And while there is a certain thrill in performing with a large group, he enjoys life most when he is performing solo on the piano for an appreciative audience.

Kristina DeShee Magelky, began journaling many years ago during the angsty years of high school and hasn't stopped writing since. In experimenting with honing her craft, DeShee has enjoyed many forms of writing such as poetry, short stories, fanfiction, and role-playing. A few of her pieces of poetry and short essays have been published, but this is the first time she has written for a group project and is honored to be a part of it. Kristina also designed the cover art for this novel.

When DeShee isn't at her day job working with special needs children in Tomball ISD, she is usually found writing, dancing, gaming, dabbling in other areas of the arts, or simply spending time with her wonderful husband and daughter.

Dean Larson has had a life filled with interesting people of all stripes. In the twenty-five years he spent counseling addicts and their families in hospitals, mental institutions, mental health centers, a prison, and finally, in his own outpatient treatment facility, he ran groups and counseled convicts and clergy, adolescents and elderly, wealthy and impoverished. The settings did much to break down class distinctions, and taught him to see people rather than titles. He learned to love people as unique individuals, whether addicted, mentally ill, behaviorally-challenged, or just down on their luck.

Dean had a side career in music that ranged from playing lead guitar in a trio that performed primarily in dark smelly bars, to performing symphonic music as "principle last trombone" in a regional symphony orchestra.

Dean hails from a family who was in love with language and the magic of words. Dinnertime conversations, when he was a child, were often discussions of philosophy or theology or books. It was there that he learned to appreciate the music and sounds, rhythm and color in words. However, he was engrossed in the mending of broken lives, and had little time for anything but professional writing. Until now.

After all the years of storing up things to express, the Tomball Community Library Writing Project offered him a gift: a chance for him to put it all on paper for others to read. Dean's efforts in this project have been done with gratitude and great anticipation for more writing.

In his travels, Ramal Anglin deals with nefarious situations and people on a daily basis. His criminal encounters often creatively find their way into his writing, and is his way of letting off steam. Therefore, when he writes, Ramal always uses a pseudonym.

When reading for pleasure, Ramal enjoys stories with strategy. Criminal justice in murder mysteries and thrillers, are right up his alley, and he treats them like his work away from work.

During a short stint at home in Tomball, he heard about the community novel at the library from one of the staff members. He joined the project, and thought it was a cool way to "kill" time between destinations.

For information about other Tomball Community Writing projects, visit:

https://tomcomwp.wixsite.com/mysite

CPSIA information can be obtained
at www.ICGtesting.com
Printed in the USA
LVHW091342240919
632114LV00001B/7/P